ENSNARED HEARTS

ANNA STONE

© 2020 Anna Stone

All rights reserved. No part of this publication may be replicated, reproduced, or redistributed in any form without the prior written consent of the publisher.

This is a work of fiction. Names, characters, places, and incidents either are the products of the author's imagination or are used fictitiously. Any resemblance to actual persons, living or dead, businesses, companies, events, or locales is entirely coincidental.

Cover by Kasmit Covers

ISBN: 9780648419273

CHAPTER 1

Kat turned on the copier and folded her arms over her chest, waiting as it whirred to life. Her gaze drifted around the Mistress Media offices, an endless expanse of glass through which more than a hundred people flowed.

She was a month into her internship at Mistress Media. After finishing grad school, she'd applied for a dozen intern positions. She'd gotten a handful of offers, but the decision to take the paid internship at Mistress Media was easy. An international media empire run by a group of the wealthiest, most successful businesswomen in the country? Mistress was the place for her.

At least, that was what she'd thought. Her internship was proving to be far less exciting than anticipated. She'd expected action-packed business meetings, dramatic negotiations, a look behind the curtain at the inner workings of a multi-billion-dollar company. Instead, Kat was stuck making coffee runs and copies day after day. She was occasionally given something more interesting to do, but that was rare, and she had to compete with all the other interns for the chance to be assigned the more challenging tasks. The Mistress office was huge, with a dozen others in the internship program all hoping to make enough of an impression to earn a permanent position. Standing out was difficult.

Kat fed a document into the copier and pressed start. She looked up at the clock on the wall. It was afternoon, but with the long hours she worked, she was barely halfway through her workday.

Her phone buzzed in her pocket. She looked around surreptitiously, then took it out. It was a message from Meghan, her roommate.

I have Friday night off. We're going out for drinks.

Kat frowned. It hadn't escaped her notice that Meghan's invitation wasn't a request. Meghan worked at a bar and her schedule was erratic, so it was rare that she had a night off to spend with Kat.

But that wasn't why Meghan was so determined to get Kat to come out with her.

She typed out a reply. *Just drinks? Or are you trying to get me to meet someone?* Kat wasn't exactly a party person, but Meghan was always trying to drag her to things. And every time, Meghan ended up acting as her unwanted wing-woman.

Meghan's reply came through instantly, as if she'd been expecting Kat's question. *Just drinks. But if you happen to meet someone, that's a bonus.*

Kat sighed. Meghan was so predictable. Before she could reply, another message from her roommate came through.

Come on. You can't stay at home and mope forever.

She put her phone in her pocket without responding. Meghan had a point. Kat had become a bit of a hermit lately.

But she had a good reason. That reason was her ex-girlfriend. It had been months since Kat had caught Brooke cheating on her, months since Kat had packed her bags and moved out of their shared apartment and into Meghan's place without so much as a word to Brooke.

Kat never wanted to see her again. But the two of them had been together since high school, and they had plenty of mutual friends. Plus, it was like every lesbian in the entire city knew each other. At any social event, she ran the risk of running into her ex-girlfriend. It was easier to just avoid them in the first place.

And she wasn't moping, despite what Meghan thought. Kat had no reason to mope. She wasn't heartbroken. As far as she was concerned, finding out the truth about her ex was a good thing. It had saved her from wasting any more of her life with Brooke.

Plus, Kat was free now, free to explore all her dreams and desires without anyone holding her back. Brooke had been her high school sweetheart, and Kat was beginning to feel like she hadn't changed at all since they'd gotten together. She'd never had the chance to grow, to experience life and be adventurous, to figure out who she really was. And now she could do just that. This was an opportunity.

At least, that was what Kat told herself so she'd feel a little less miserable.

She looked at Meghan's message again. Perhaps she did need to get back into the dating scene. It had been months since everything with Brooke, and although Kat was certainly done with relationships, something casual wasn't out of the question. A one-night stand, a fling, maybe? She wanted to be adventurous, after all.

There was one problem—her lack of experience with women. She'd only ever been with Brooke, and like most high school relationships, it had just happened. She'd never even flirted with someone or asked someone out. She didn't know how.

On the other hand, she needed something, anything, to spice up her dull life.

She replied to Meghan. *Fine, I'll come. But only to get you off my back.*

She put her phone away and checked the copier. It was barely halfway done. She fiddled with her light brown curls, tucking one back into the high bun she'd attempted to restrain her hair in.

As her eyes wandered around the office once more, she spotted a woman who stood out from everyone else. She stood by the interns' desks, speaking with the internship supervisor. Her auburn hair was pulled back into a sleek ponytail, and she was dressed in a white collared blouse, a black skirt, and heels. It was a simple outfit, but on her it looked anything but plain. Her fine clothing was tailored to fit her body perfectly, the tight pencil skirt accentuating her slender hips, the heels making her lean legs look endless.

Lydia Davenport. She was one of the five women who ran Mistress Media, Mistress's new CFO. Kat had only interacted with her a dozen times. Lydia would occasionally give one of the interns a task to do, and every time Lydia chose her, Kat would get flustered in her presence, blushing and tripping over her words.

To say she had a crush was an understatement. Lydia was powerful, successful, mysterious, not to mention gorgeous. She simply dripped glamor and elegance. She was the kind of woman Kat only fantasized about.

And given how much of Kat's workday was spent on mindless tasks, she had plenty of time to fantasize about Lydia. She'd imagine Lydia calling her into her office, late at night, when everyone else had gone home and they were all alone. What happened next depended on how creative Kat was feeling, but it usually involved Lydia kissing Kat on her desk.

Kat's cheeks grew hot. She turned back to the photocopier. She needed to focus. She should not have been thinking that way about Lydia Davenport. Not only was Lydia her superior, but Kat doubted the woman even knew she existed.

Suddenly, the copier made a loud clanking sound, then stopped. Kat let out a frustrated sigh. *Again?* It was like she spent half her workday dealing with copier malfunctions.

As she opened the side of the machine and bent over to inspect it, she heard the click of heeled footsteps approaching. At the same time, the sweet scent of expensive perfume filled the air.

The footsteps stopped behind her.

"Katherine. I've been looking for you."

Kat froze. She would recognize that smooth, soft, but oh-so-commanding voice anywhere. She turned around, her heart racing.

Lydia Davenport stood before her, looking even more alluring up close than she did in Kat's daydreams. Her lips were a deep shade of red, and her high cheekbones were tinged with the suggestion of pink.

Kat looked around. There was no one else nearby. Lydia was talking to *her*? And she knew Kat's name?

"It *is* Katherine, isn't it?" Lydia asked. "Do you prefer Kate?"

"I… I usually go by Kat," she replied. "But you can call me whatever you want." *Oh my god, did I just say that out loud?*

A hint of amusement flashed behind Lydia's blue-gray eyes. "Kat it is."

Kat willed herself to sink into the floor. When that didn't work, she pulled herself together, enough to speak at least.

"You were looking for me?" Lydia probably had a task for her to do. It was still unusual that she had sought Kat out personally. Usually, when she needed something done, Lydia would simply breeze by and issue the nearest intern a command without giving them a chance to ask questions.

Lydia folded her arms across her chest. "I need to borrow an intern for the afternoon, and you're the only one who seems capable of following directions."

So Kat had made an impression on Lydia, and a positive one at that? She'd had no idea.

"If you're busy, I can ask one of the other interns."

"I'm not busy," Kat said, a little too enthusiastically. "I'm just making copies. At least, I was trying to. Now I'm fixing the copier." She clamped her mouth shut. Sometimes it worked faster than her brain.

Lydia glanced at the copier disdainfully. "Having interns do these kinds of tasks is such a waste. I'm sure you didn't go to grad school so you could fix office equipment. You must be bored out of your mind."

"I don't mind," Kat lied. "Everyone has to start somewhere. I'm just grateful for the opportunity to work at Mistress."

"Such a diplomatic answer. I can see why your supervisor speaks so highly of you." Lydia looked Kat up and down. "You're the whole package."

Lydia's gaze locked with Kat's, her eyes stormy. There was something about her that left Kat mesmerized. And that was on top of the fact that Kat found her irresistibly beautiful.

"Here's what I need from you," Lydia said. "I have a meeting with the marketing team in half an hour. I need someone to take minutes for me. It's an assistant's job, but I haven't hired one yet, so you'll have to fill in. Do you think you can handle that?"

Kat nodded. "Sure. Anything you need."

"The meeting is in conference room three. Head there now and set up the projector. And we'll need refreshments."

Kat nodded. But Lydia was already walking away.

Kat let out a breath. Was she so infatuated that she forgot how to breathe when Lydia was around? She was twenty-four years old, and here she was acting like a smitten schoolgirl.

She needed to get a hold of herself. There was no chance of anything ever happening between her and Lydia Davenport.

And even if there was, after everything with her ex-girlfriend, Kat was done with women forever.

CHAPTER 2

Lydia shut her eyes, seeking respite from the glare of her laptop screen. It was late evening, and she'd planned to leave the office an hour ago, but she had too much work to do for her upcoming business trip to Paris.

For the third time that day, she made a mental note to hire an assistant. She'd been putting it off for far too long. It was entirely unlike her. But she knew exactly why she was avoiding it.

Because hiring an assistant, someone permanent, would mean that she was finally putting down roots.

She stretched out her legs and leaned back in her leather chair, surveying the wider Mistress offices through the glass walls of her executive office. As of three months ago, one-fifth of everything she could see belonged to her. She'd been working for Mistress Media as a financial consultant on an as-needed basis for several years after a mutual friend had recommended her to Mistress's CEO, Madison Sloane. Madison had offered her a full-time position several times before, but Lydia had turned her down. She didn't need the money, and she hadn't been ready to make such a significant move.

But earlier in the year, Madison made her an offer she couldn't refuse—a CFO position with a generous salary, a significant stake in the company, and a corner office. Lydia couldn't justify turning it down. She'd accepted Madison's offer, moving halfway across the country to take up the job. It had been time to start a new chapter in her life. Time to move on.

But truly moving on—from her old life, from her past, from Emily's death—was more difficult than simply moving cities.

There was a knock on Lydia's door. Lydia looked up to find Yvonne Maxwell standing in her doorway. Yvonne was Mistress's COO, and she was running the company while Madison was off on her month-long honeymoon. As far as colleagues went, Lydia liked Yvonne. She appreciated the dark-haired woman's no-nonsense attitude.

Lydia waved her inside.

"Here." Yvonne placed a stack of files on Lydia's desk. "It's everything I have on Belle Magazine, including ten years of financial reports. The older reports are available if you need them."

"This should be enough," Lydia said. "Thank you."

"I should be thanking you for going on this trip. I have my hands full with Madison away."

"It's no trouble." Lydia was looking forward to it. The purpose of the trip was to meet with the owners of Belle Magazine to negotiate an acquisition. Yvonne usually handled deals like these, but Lydia had offered to go instead.

She spoke some French, and although she wasn't fluent, it would make communicating easier.

"If there's anything else you need to make this deal happen, let me know," Yvonne said. "Acquiring Belle is vital to our plan to open a Mistress office in Paris. And it will get the board off our backs about focusing on more profitable ventures. That sex-positive women's blog we acquired isn't exactly going to be lucrative, but a prestigious female-run fashion magazine fits our mission statement *and* it has the potential to be profitable."

Lydia was well aware of the importance of the Belle deal. Although Mistress's finances were solid, because of Madison's insistence on not compromising the company's mission statement, profits weren't where the shareholders wanted them to be. It was causing conflict between the board and the executive team.

Madison's answer to that had been to hire Lydia. She felt that Mistress needed someone with an eye for finance. The board disagreed, calling Lydia's hiring an unnecessary expense. Lydia was determined to prove her worth.

"You have nothing to worry about," Lydia said. "I'll take care of everything."

"I have no doubt you will," Yvonne said. "And if you want some help on your trip, feel free to take one of the interns with you."

"That's an excellent idea." Without an assistant, Lydia could use the extra hands.

"Let me know if you need anything else." Yvonne looked at her watch. "I'm due to meet the others for a late dinner. It was a last-minute thing. Would you like to join us?"

"The others" referred to the rest of the executive team.

They were a tight-knit group, friends from long before they'd started Mistress Media. Lydia was the only one of them who hadn't been with the company from the start. They were all nice enough, but Lydia had never been much of a team player. She preferred to keep to herself.

Besides, she already had plans for the night. "Unfortunately, I'll have to pass. I have plans of my own."

Yvonne nodded. "All right. I'll see you tomorrow."

As Yvonne left the room, Lydia flipped through the files Yvonne had left, but her mind had already checked out. She placed the files to the side and began packing up her desk. It was Thursday, almost the end of the week, and Lydia was feeling the need to unwind, to escape. She had a very specific way of doing that.

But first, she needed to get ready.

Lydia walked to the door of her office and pressed a button beside it. Like magic, the surrounding glass walls dimmed to opaque. The modern, all-glass design of the Mistress offices provided little privacy, but fortunately, the executives' offices were equipped with this function.

She returned to her desk and grabbed her Italian leather duffel bag from the bottom drawer. She unzipped the bag, pulled out a black, damask-patterned corset, and slipped it on over her blouse, cinching it tightly around her waist. She reached into the bag again and produced a pair of stiletto heels, swapping her more practical work pumps out for them.

She inspected herself in the mirror she'd installed inside the door of the cabinet in the corner, straightening out her blouse under the corset and smoothing down her skirt. The look was simple, but it got the message across. She'd never been the type for full-body leather.

For a finishing touch, Lydia took her lipstick from her purse and applied it to her lips, turning them a deep, dark crimson, then she slipped her coat on and buttoned it up.

Grabbing her duffel bag, Lydia left her office. As she made her way toward the elevators, she spotted Kat sitting at the interns' desks, her curl-covered head buried in her laptop.

Lydia would have to take an intern to Paris with her, and she needed to decide who to take before the week ended. Kat was the obvious choice. She worked the hardest of all the interns, and she was always so eager to please. Whenever Lydia called upon her, Kat would appear instantly, as if she'd been waiting for her the entire time.

As Lydia approached, Kat peered up from her laptop. Her eyes traveled down Lydia's body all the way to her stiletto heels. Her lips parted slightly, but no sound emerged.

Lydia slowed her pace, stopping before Kat's desk. "Goodnight, Kat."

Kat's eyes flicked up to Lydia's. "Goodnight," she murmured.

They held each other's gazes. And for a moment, Lydia couldn't help but wonder—did Kat's eagerness to impress go beyond her job? When Lydia had praised her for how good she was at following instructions, her cheeks had turned a delectable shade of pink, and her amber eyes had lit up with something far more than satisfaction.

And how tantalizing that had been.

But Kat was an intern. Lydia shouldn't have been

thinking about an employee that way, let alone one so much younger than her.

Giving Kat a cordial nod, Lydia swept off toward the elevators.

If she wanted an escape, she would have to get it elsewhere.

Lydia entered the darkened club. Although it was a weeknight, the exclusive, high-end venue was busy. The kind of people who frequented the club were looking for a specific, unconventional kind of escape, one they took very seriously.

Lilith's Den was one of the few places in the city where they could find that escape. The club was the height of opulence, catering only to the wealthiest of clientele. But more importantly, it was a place people could go to live out their darkest, most twisted desires.

All around her, people were doing just that. Nearby, a woman led another around on a leash while wielding a long, thin whip. On a stage at the end of the room, a woman was slowly being bound from head to toe.

This was Lydia's world. Although the club itself was new to her, the world it represented was one she was intimately familiar with. She was in her element here.

She took a seat in a plush chaise lounge at the side of the room. Almost immediately, a waitress came by and offered Lydia her usual glass of champagne. She'd become a regular at the club since moving here. Whenever she felt the need to unwind, she would come to Lilith's Den to find an eager, willing submissive who wanted nothing more than to surrender to Lydia for a night, sometimes longer. More often than not, there was no sex involved. It wasn't about sex. It was simply a way for her to lose herself.

But lately, she wasn't finding it as satisfying as she used to. Something was missing. Could it be that she craved something more than physical? After all, the kinky power games that she enjoyed were the most satisfying when the connection between those involved ran deeper.

Lydia had never had that with anyone other than Emily. The love of her life. Her wife.

But three years ago, Lydia had buried Emily. And Lydia's heart was buried with her.

That was why Lydia came to places like this, why she sought the escape she did. After Emily's death, Lydia had hardened herself. She'd numbed herself to the pain and hopelessness she'd felt, embracing strength, power, and control instead. She sought refuge in the familiar, putting on a mask, letting her Domme side take over.

Over time, she'd found herself wearing that mask twenty-four seven.

As she sipped her champagne, Lydia noticed a woman trying to catch her eye. She kept glancing in Lydia's direction before looking away demurely. The woman wouldn't dare to approach. This was Lydia's domain. Here, she called the shots. If she wanted to, she could have the woman—or half the other women in the club—kneeling at her feet with little more than a look.

But Lydia wasn't interested in her, or anyone else in the club.

Was it a sign she was finally ready to move on from

Emily? Sure, Lydia had already taken steps toward doing so. She'd accepted the job at Mistress. She'd put their old house outside Chicago up for sale. She'd bought a new apartment here in the city.

She wanted to move on. She wanted more than a life of grief and memories.

Yet, she struggled to leave the past behind.

She wasn't truly ready to move on from Emily. Perhaps she never would be.

As Lydia let her gaze wander around the club, her eyes landed on another woman, one with light brown curly hair, a subtle collar-style choker adorning her neck. She was tall and willowy instead of short with minute curves, yet Lydia's mind went straight to a certain intern.

Kat.

Why was Lydia seeing Kat's face here and now? Eager Kat, always coming at Lydia's beck and call. Everything about her was so enticing. Her honeyed voice. Her light brown curls, which she would play with whenever Lydia was near. Her shimmering gold eyes, which would linger on Lydia's for just a touch too long.

A thought slipped into Lydia's mind. *Would Kat be out of place at a place like this?*

Lydia drained her champagne and got up from her seat. She wasn't going to find what she was looking for here, not tonight. And clearly, she was too preoccupied with work, considering she couldn't get her mind off Kat.

As she made her way to the door, she made a mental note to ask Kat to come to Paris with her first thing in the morning.

CHAPTER 3

Kat dragged herself into work the next morning, ready for another day of coffee runs and copier malfunctions. It was Friday, and she couldn't wait until the weekend. She was actually looking forward to going out with Meghan for drinks.

She headed to her desk. She was early, but predictably, one other intern had already arrived. Sitting at the desk across from Kat's was a dark-haired, dark-eyed woman drinking from an enormous cup of coffee. Courtney.

She and Kat had gone to grad school together. Courtney had been the perfect student, and now she was the perfect intern. She'd always been highly competitive, and a bit of a teacher's pet. She was no different as an intern. She wouldn't have to worry about not getting a permanent position here at Mistress after their internship ended.

Spotting Kat, Courtney waved. Before Kat had a chance to say hi, Courtney pointed to Kat's desk. "There's a note for you. It's from Lydia. She wants to see you."

Courtney also had a tendency to be nosy. That hadn't changed since grad school either.

Kat took a seat at her desk and picked up the note.

Come see me when you get in. I'll be in my office.

The note was signed with Lydia's name.

Courtney peered around her monitor at Kat. "What does she want with you?"

Kat didn't miss the hint of jealousy in Courtney's voice. "I have no idea." Before yesterday, Kat had thought Lydia didn't even know who she was, and now she was personally summoning Kat to her office? "I guess I'll go find out."

She left her desk and headed to Lydia's office. The door was open. Still, Kat knocked on it tentatively.

"Come in," Lydia said, not looking up at her. "And shut the door."

Kat closed the door and entered the room. The spacious corner office was cleanly furnished, with a large glass desk that matched the walls and a small black leather couch and coffee table by the window. The Mistress offices were on the top floor of the building, and the view outside the windows was spectacular.

She inched toward Lydia's desk. She was alone with Lydia in her office, just like in all those daydreams of hers. Sure, anyone walking by could see inside, but that didn't stop Kat's mind from filling with all kinds of indecent scenarios.

Lydia shut her laptop and pushed it aside, then leaned back in her leather chair, studying Kat silently. Her penetrating gaze made Kat feel like Lydia could see all those images going through her mind. She willed herself not to blush. It didn't work.

Finally, Lydia spoke. "Do you have a current passport?"

Kat nodded. "Yes." She'd never actually used it. She'd been planning a trip to South America with her ex-girlfriend before they'd broken up.

"Good. You're coming to Paris with me next week."

Kat blinked. "I am?"

"If you can't come, I can ask one of the other interns."

"No. Yes, I can come," Kat said quickly. "But why do you want me to go with you?"

"I'm sure you've heard talk of Mistress's plans to open our first international office in Paris?"

Kat nodded. She'd heard rumors along those lines, but she didn't know the details. After all, she was just an intern.

"There's a French publishing company we're looking to acquire that will make the perfect foundation for our European portfolio. They publish Belle Magazine. I'm going to meet with the owners to negotiate a deal, and while I'm in the city, I'm going to lay the groundwork for establishing Mistress Paris. I have a packed schedule. I'm going to need an assistant. Since I haven't hired one yet, I decided to take an intern with me instead."

"Right. Okay."

Lydia examined her. "You meant why did I pick you and not one of the other interns."

Kat nodded.

"It's simple. Of all the interns, you're the most competent. You stand out from all the rest. Does that surprise you?"

"A little. I didn't think you'd noticed me at all." Kat fidgeted with one of her curls. She really needed to keep her thoughts to herself.

"Of course I've noticed you. How could I not?" Lydia leaned forward and crossed her arms, resting them on her glass desk. "Like I said yesterday, you've proven you can follow instructions well. You're exactly what I'm looking for."

Kat's cheeks grew warm, a wave of heat coming over her. That seemed to happen a lot whenever she was around Lydia.

"Now, back to the trip," Lydia said. "We'll be in Paris Monday to Friday. Our flight leaves Sunday night. I'll send you our schedule as well as some materials for you to read before the trip. Mistress's plan for the international expansion, information on Belle Magazine. I need you to get up to speed before the trip."

Kat nodded mutely. Was this really happening? Was she going to Paris?

"Do you have any questions?" Lydia asked.

Kat found her voice again. "No."

"If anything comes up, just ask." Lydia opened her laptop up again, resuming her work.

Kat left Lydia's office, her stomach fluttering with excitement. She was going to Paris, one of the most beautiful, romantic cities in the world. Sure, it was for a work trip, but she'd never even left the country for any reason.

And in just a few days, she'd be on her way to France with Lydia Davenport, a woman she'd been infatuated with since the day she'd first laid eyes on her.

She took a seat at her desk. She needed to focus on what was important. This trip was an opportunity for Kat to impress Lydia. Kat's internship was temporary. At the end of it, Mistress would only hire a select few of the interns permanently, and Kat was determined to be one of them. This was her chance to stand out.

Kat checked her inbox. Sure enough, there was already an email from Lydia with half a dozen documents attached. There had to be hundreds of pages. And Kat was supposed to read everything before Monday?

She sighed. Even if she started now, she was going to have to spend the entire weekend reading, and she was going to have to work late tonight.

But it would all be worth it.

When Kat got home that night, she found her roommate on the couch, watching TV. Meghan was dressed in sweats, her short, dark hair hidden under her hoodie.

"Hey, Meghan." Kat collapsed on the couch next to her. "I had the craziest day."

Meghan said nothing, her eyes remaining fixed on the TV.

Kat frowned. "What's the matter?"

Meghan crossed her arms. "Did you forget about something?"

"What do you-" Kat groaned. "Drinks. That was tonight. I'm so sorry. Something came up at work and I completely forgot."

"Sure," Meghan muttered. "Whatever."

"It's true. I got asked to go on a business trip next week. I just have so much to do, and I completely forgot we had plans. I should have messaged you and canceled."

"I'm not upset because you forgot to cancel. I'm upset

because you blew me off in the first place. This isn't the first time."

Kat felt a pang of guilt. "I know, and I'm sorry. But I have a good excuse. The CFO herself asked me to go with her to Paris next week. I needed to stay late to prepare. I'm going to spend most of the weekend preparing too."

"Fine, I'll give you a pass this time. But next time, you're not getting out of it. You can't spend the rest of your life holed up at home."

"What are you, my mom?" Kat muttered.

"No, I'm the one who has to put up with you sulking around the apartment whenever you're not at work. You're stuck in this rut, and you're doing nothing to get yourself out of it."

Kat couldn't deny that she tended to be passive when it came to her problems, but Meghan was making a big deal out of nothing. "I haven't been sulking. And I'm totally fine."

"No, you're not. I'm starting to worry about you. Ever since everything with you-know-who, you've been so withdrawn."

Kat crossed her arms. "You can say her name, you know. And sure, maybe I have been moping a little. But what do you expect? My girlfriend of almost ten years cheated on me. I lost most of my friends because of it. My entire life was upended. That's not something you just get over."

"I know. But you can't go on like this forever." Meghan's expression softened. "I'm starting to miss the old Kat."

"I'm still the same old Kat. And I appreciate your concern, but I'm fine. Really."

Meghan gave her a skeptical look. "If you say so."

Kat sighed. "How about this? Next time there's something you want me to go to with you, I'm in. I promise."

"Okay, but I'm going to hold you to that."

"That's fine with me."

Meghan stretched out on the couch lazily. "So, Paris, huh?"

"Yeah, it's pretty exciting. I doubt I'll get to do anything fun, though. Something tells me Lydia isn't going to give me a minute of free time."

Meghan raised an eyebrow. "Lydia?"

"She's Mistress's CFO. I'm going on the trip as her assistant."

"Oh, she's the one you have a crush on."

"I didn't say that." What Kat had said was that she found Lydia attractive. It had slipped out when she'd been telling Meghan about her internship. "But yes, it's her."

"Lucky you. Even if you end up working the whole trip, at least you get to spend it with a total babe." Meghan gave her a sly smile. "All that time together, just the two of you? Who knows what will happen?"

Kat put her hands on her hips. "She's my boss, Meghan! That would be totally inappropriate." Yet, Kat had had so many inappropriate thoughts about Lydia.

Meghan chuckled. "Relax, I'm just teasing you. It's cute how much of a prude you are."

"Just because I don't jump into bed with every woman who looks my way doesn't make me a prude." Meghan wasn't shy about her exploits when it came to women.

"I don't sleep with *every* woman who looks my way. If I did, I'd have no spare time."

Kat rolled her eyes. But Meghan had a point. Kat and

Lydia would be working together closely all week, and Kat was as excited about that part of the trip as she was nervous. Five whole days in a foreign country with a woman who rendered her breathless every time she walked by?

Kat hoped she'd be able to keep it together.

CHAPTER 4

The seatbelt light blinked off. Lydia unbuckled her seatbelt and stretched out in the spacious, first class seat. The flight was a long one, so she was keen to settle in and get comfortable. A glass of wine would help with that.

She turned to Kat, who was sitting beside her, gazing around at everything wide-eyed.

"First time flying?" Lydia asked.

Kat shook her head. "Just my first time in first class."

"First class certainly makes these long flights more enjoyable. Mistress got rid of the private jet for environmental reasons, so this will have to do."

"This is more than fine," Kat said.

A moment later, a flight attendant came by.

"Bonjour, my name is Michael." The man spoke with a heavy French accent. "I will be looking after you during this flight. Can I offer you some refreshments?"

Lydia inquired about the selection of wines available, kicking off a lengthy conversation. Wine was one of Lydia's passions. Whenever she visited France, she took full advantage of the excellent wines the country had to offer.

After some discussion, she settled on a pinot noir from Burgundy.

"Excellent choix." Michael turned to Kat. "Et pour vous, mademoiselle?"

Kat stared back at him blankly. It took Lydia a moment to realize she'd slipped into French while speaking with him.

"Elle ne parle pas français," Lydia said to the man. She turned back to Kat. "He asked what you'd like."

"Nothing for me," Kat said.

"Are you sure?"

"I'm all right."

"It's an eight-hour flight," Lydia said. "If you want something, ask for it. It will make the flight much more pleasant. Besides, Mistress is paying for everything."

"Okay. Sure."

"I'm getting the pinot noir. I highly recommend it."

"I don't really know much about wine," Kat admitted.

Lydia thought for a moment. "Do you drink champagne?"

Kat nodded.

"Then we'll have that instead." Lydia turned to Michael and requested a bottle of champagne for them to share. It was a long flight, after all.

As the flight attendant disappeared down the aisle, Lydia noticed Kat's gaze on her. As she met Kat's eyes, Kat glanced away.

"What is it?" Lydia asked.

"Nothing," Kat said quickly. "I just didn't know you spoke French. It sounds so beautiful. The language, I mean."

"It really is a beautiful language. But I only speak a touch."

"That sounded like more than a touch."

"I'm far from fluent, but I lived in France for a while, so I picked up some French."

Kat sighed wistfully. "I'd love to live in France. Did you live in Paris?"

"I lived farther south, in the countryside." Lydia and Emily had had a villa there. This was the first time she'd been back to France since Emily had passed. It was bittersweet.

She pushed the feeling aside. "Before we land, I'll teach you a few words of French. It's always useful to know the basics, and it's good manners to make an effort to learn the local language when traveling. Now, did you do all the reading I gave you?"

Kat nodded.

"I want to hear what you took away from it. Tell me, why does Mistress want to acquire Belle Magazine?"

Kat thought for a moment. "For starters, Mistress has acquired several international publications over the past few years, but nothing in Europe. Belle will give Mistress a foothold in the European market. And they're perfect for Mistress in terms of their vision. The company is female-led, and the magazine is notable for its articles on more serious subjects in between all the fashion content. Their audience is the same as ours."

"It seems you did your homework," Lydia said. "But Belle

is clearly struggling. Why is Mistress interested in a company that's facing bankruptcy?"

Kat's response was instant. "The reason Belle is failing is that they haven't kept up with the changing media landscape. If they were to shift the focus from print to online, it would draw in a larger audience, not to mention a younger one. That's what I'd do if I was in charge."

"Very good. That's an interesting strategy."

"I didn't think of it myself. It's what Mistress did a couple of years ago with Q Magazine, as well as a few others."

Lydia studied Kat's face. "That wasn't in the notes I gave you."

"No, but I did my research on Mistress long before I even applied for the internship. I read everything I could find on the company. I noticed certain trends when it came to the companies Mistress has acquired over the last few years."

Lydia shouldn't have been surprised by Kat's thoroughness. Kat was a contradiction sometimes. When speaking about anything work-related, she was confident and self-assured, but whenever Lydia spoke to her about anything else, Kat was liable to start blushing and stammering. Was it Lydia herself that had that effect on her?

Noticing Lydia's stare, Kat frowned. "Did I say something wrong?"

"I'm impressed, that's all," Lydia said. "It seems I was right when I said you're capable of far more than fixing the copier."

"Well, I don't have much practical experience, but I've

learned a lot. I'm ready to put it all into use, to show you what I can do."

"So eager. I like that." Lydia folded her arms across her chest. "So that's why you were so keen to come to Paris with me? You wanted to impress me?"

Kat's cheeks flushed pink. "Yes, for the sake of my internship. The program is really competitive."

A smile pulled at Lydia's lips. "I'm sure it is."

"Well, there's another reason I wanted to come on this trip. I've always wanted to visit Paris. Seeing it is a dream come true."

"I should warn you, you won't get any time for sightseeing. Our schedule is packed. I'm afraid this trip will be all work and no play."

"I know. But I'm grateful that I get to see Paris all the same."

The flight attendant returned with a bottle of champagne and two glasses. He set them down on the table between them before pouring them each a glass, then stood by and waited for Lydia to sample it.

"Merci." Lydia picked up the glass, breathing in the sweet aroma before tasting it. It was excellent.

Lydia gave Michael a nod of approval. He instructed them to let him know if they needed anything before disappearing down the aisle.

Lydia turned to Kat, gesturing toward Kat's glass. "Aren't you going to try it?"

Kat picked up her champagne and took a sip. Her eyes lit up. "This is great."

"There's more where that came from. I ordered the whole bottle. Just ask Michael if you want another glass."

Kat glanced down at her champagne. "Drinking champagne on work time feels a little weird."

"Like I said, it's a long flight. Why not indulge a little? I certainly plan to." Lydia lowered her voice. "Let's be a little naughty. I won't tell if you won't."

A coy smile crossed Kat's lips. "Sure."

As Kat lifted the glass to her mouth again, Lydia's eyes were drawn to her lips. They were full and pink, glistening with the remnants of champagne. Kat set down her glass and let out a satisfied sigh, then reached behind her head and tugged her curls out of their ponytail. Lydia watched out the corner of her eye as Kat shook her hair out and ran her fingers through it, letting her curls settle on her shoulders. With her hair down, her curls framed her face in the most inviting way…

Lydia tore her eyes away. She couldn't let her mind go there. If there was anyone who was off-limits, it was Kat. Mixing work with pleasure was never a good idea. Not to mention, Kat essentially worked for her. Lydia couldn't abuse her position of power.

But would Lydia really be taking advantage? Kat's attraction to her was obvious in every word she spoke, in every glance.

They were both adults, weren't they?

Lydia banished the thought from her mind and reached for her bag, taking out her laptop from it. "I'm going to get some work done while I can. We arrive at midday Paris time, so be sure to get some sleep."

Kat nodded. "All right."

Lydia opened up her laptop, focusing her mind on work. Was she going to regret bringing Kat to Paris? She hadn't considered how maddening it was going to be to spend a week with a woman she found irresistible but couldn't possibly touch.

Because getting involved with an intern wasn't just a bad idea. It could put Lydia's job at risk. Her position as CFO was hardly secure. It was never a good look for an executive to have any kind of relationship with an employee, so if things went south, there would be consequences. The board was hostile to her already, and she wasn't going to give them an excuse to oust her. It had taken Lydia so long to decide to accept the job in the first place. She couldn't risk losing it.

That should have been enough to get the idea of pursuing Kat right out of Lydia's head.

But it only made Lydia want her even more.

CHAPTER 5

Kat awoke on Tuesday morning, bleary-eyed and in dire need of coffee. It was her second day in Paris, and she was already exhausted. Not only was jet lag setting in, but the moment she and Lydia had stepped off the plane on Monday, they'd rushed from meeting to meeting without so much as a minute to breathe in between. Lydia hadn't been kidding when she'd said that the trip would be all work and no play.

As she finished getting dressed, room service arrived with her breakfast. She wolfed it down as fast as she could. She didn't have long until they were due to leave, so she didn't have time to enjoy the lavish meal. She hadn't had the chance to enjoy any of the other comforts that came with her luxury hotel room either. Her five-star accommodations were more extravagant than any hotel she'd ever stayed at, and Lydia had told her to help herself to whatever she needed, all at Mistress's expense. If she wanted to, she could summon someone to give her a massage, or to draw her a bath, to procure her anything she desired.

It seemed Lydia liked to travel in style. Kat certainly wasn't complaining.

Ten minutes later Kat was out the door. As she shut it behind her, Lydia emerged from the room next to hers. Lydia was always pure style, but she was dressed even more fashionably than usual in a red shift dress, belted to accentuate her figure, and shiny black heels. If she was jet-lagged, it didn't show. Her unshakable confidence was as apparent as ever.

How did Lydia always manage to look so impossibly perfect? Kat resisted the urge to blurt the thought out. She was doing a terrible job of keeping her crush on Lydia in check. Despite having spent the last day and a half with her, Kat still couldn't help but feel flustered in her presence.

It took Kat a moment to notice that Lydia was staring at her, her lips pursed.

"Is everything okay?" Kat asked.

"Is this what you're wearing today?" Lydia said.

Kat looked down at her outfit. "Is there something wrong with it?" Today, like most workdays, she'd dressed in a blouse paired with a black skirt and flats. She wasn't the type to care about fashion. As long as she looked presentable and her hair was cooperating, she was happy.

"Do you know what we're doing this evening?"

Kat nodded. "The meeting with the owners of Belle Magazine." It was a dinner meeting, which, according to Lydia, was the perfect way to build rapport with business contacts.

"Yes, and Belle is primarily a fashion magazine. When we meet the owners tonight, we need to show them that their company will be in good hands with us. We need to make a good impression, which means looking the part."

"Right." Kat pulled at the sleeve of her blouse. "It's just, I don't have anything else to wear."

"That's easy enough to fix." Lydia looked at her watch. "What do we have scheduled for this morning?"

Kat went through the schedule she'd memorized in her head. "At 9 a.m. you have an appointment with the realtor to inspect potential locations for a Mistress Paris office. After that is a meeting with some potential investors at eleven."

"Call the realtor and reschedule for tomorrow evening. That will give us more than enough time."

"Enough time for what?"

Lydia had already started toward the elevator. "Come along. We're going shopping."

Fifteen minutes and a cab ride later, Kat found herself standing on a Paris street, boutique fashion stores stretching as far as the eye could see. She looked around, entranced as women strolled by, the height of sophistication in elegant coats and stylish heels, their hair and makeup done to perfection.

This was the image of Paris that Kat had had in her head.

Lydia gestured around them. "This is Triangle d'Or, the home of Paris's finest haute couture. There's no better place to find you something to wear than here."

Kat glanced down the street. The signs above the stores were all high-end brands, most of which she'd only ever heard of. Dior. Prada. Gucci. Other stores bore names that were entirely unfamiliar to her. Everything was bound to be way out of her price range.

"Is something the matter?" Lydia asked.

"I don't think I can afford anything from these stores," Kat admitted.

"Lucky for you, you're not the one paying for any of it." Lydia continued down the street, looking back over her shoulder at Kat. "Come along, we don't have time to stand around."

Kat followed her. Was she going to charge this to the company like the flight and the hotel room, or was she paying for it herself? Kat didn't think designer clothing for an intern counted as a business expense.

"Here we are." Lydia stopped in front of a nondescript store. "I haven't been here in years, but this boutique always had an excellent selection of curated pieces."

Lydia opened the door and waltzed purposefully into the store. Kat followed at her heels. The shop was small but well stocked, showcasing several pieces on mannequins, each of them ornate and intricately designed.

"We don't have much time," Lydia said. "I'm going to look around, try to find something appropriate. You should do the same."

Kat nodded. As Lydia headed toward the opposite end of the store, Kat reached for a nearby rack and pulled out a garment at random, a shapeless asymmetrical tunic so short that Kat couldn't tell if it was a dress or a blouse. This was "haute couture"?

Kat looked at the tag. Predictably, there was no price on

it, which had to mean that it was extremely expensive. She put the tunic back and looked around the boutique some more. How was she supposed to find something 'appropriate' when she didn't even know what to look for?

Her eyes fell on a mannequin in the center of the room. It was clad in a short black cocktail dress with long sleeves and a plunging neckline. The dress was made of several layers of sheer fabric, giving it a floaty, translucent appearance.

It was beautiful.

Kat reached up to it, letting her fingertips graze the delicate fabric. The dress wasn't the kind of thing she'd ever wear, even if she'd had an occasion for something so elegant. And yet, she was enchanted by it. What would it feel like to wear something like this, the soft, light fabric hugging her body?

"Est-ce que je peux vous aider?"

Kat turned to see a woman looking back at her with a frown. A sales assistant? The woman's narrowed eyes flicked down Kat's body, taking in the cheap blouse and skirt Kat wore, her nose screwed up with disdain.

Kat pulled her hand away from the dress. What had the woman said to her? She could barely remember the few words of French that Lydia had taught her. She glanced around, trying to catch Lydia's eye, but Lydia was busy flicking through the racks at the other side of the store, a few pieces of clothing slung over one arm.

The woman scoffed. "A tourist?" She muttered something under her breath in exasperated French. "I'll say it again. Can I help you?"

"Um, I'm just looking for…"

"Just looking." The woman crossed her arms. "This is not a museum. These clothes aren't here to be looked at or touched. If you want to go around touching things, I suggest you go somewhere more… affordable."

Kat's ears burned. As she racked her brains for a response, she felt a hand on her shoulder.

Lydia.

Kat turned to look at her. Lydia was staring at the saleswoman, her lips pressed together in a straight line, her face clouding over.

She spoke with a firmness that sent a shiver down the back of Kat's neck. "Is there a problem here, Kat?"

"No." It was a lie, but with Lydia touching her, Kat was finding it hard to form sentences.

The saleswoman looked Lydia up and down, her frown transforming into a smile. But before she could say a single word, Lydia cut her off, speaking to her in French, her tone as sharp as her gaze.

The woman glanced at Kat, then back at Lydia. She replied to Lydia, her manner deferential. Kat didn't need to speak French to know that Lydia was admonishing the woman. And for whatever reason, it made Kat hot all over.

She needed to get a hold of herself.

The saleswoman turned to Kat, her hands clasped in front of her. "Je suis désolée. I'm sorry, mademoiselle. How can I be of service to you both?"

Lydia thrust the clothes she was holding into the woman's arms. "Take these to fitting room, then come back."

"Of course." The woman bobbed her head, trying but

failing to hide her sour expression. It was clear she didn't like being treated like a servant.

Lydia stared at the woman with narrowed eyes as she disappeared toward the fitting rooms. "The service has gone downhill since I was last here," she muttered. She turned to Kat, releasing her grip on Kat's shoulder, but the intensity in her eyes didn't disappear. "Are you all right? Did she make you uncomfortable? We can take our business elsewhere if you'd prefer it."

Somehow, Kat managed to find her voice. "I'm fine. And thanks. For sticking up for me and everything."

"I simply can't stand people like that." Lydia looked at the mannequin next to them, the one with the black dress. "Is this what you were looking at?"

"I thought it was pretty, that's all." Kat took one last look at the dress. "But it probably isn't right for tonight."

"It's a beautiful dress. You have excellent taste. I'm sure it would look stunning on you." Lydia's eyes skimmed down Kat's body. "But you're right, it isn't appropriate for a business dinner. Let's find you something else."

Lydia swept off toward a rack of blouses. Giving up on her own search, Kat followed her. When the saleswoman returned, Lydia handed her the clothing she was holding and continued to peruse the store, ignoring all the woman's attempts to help. Kat suspected that Lydia was relishing ordering the snobby saleswoman around. Kat was certainly enjoying it.

Finally, Lydia added a pair of slacks to the pile in the saleswoman's arms. She turned to Kat. "There. That gives us plenty of options. Go try them on."

Lydia ushered Kat to the fitting rooms. Once the saleswoman finished hanging everything up for them, Lydia gave her a sharp look.

"That will be all," she said.

The woman plastered on an entirely false smile. "Let me know if you need anything." She backed out of the fitting rooms, returning to the sales floor where she pretended not to watch them out of the corner of her eye.

Lydia gestured toward the fitting room stall, holding the curtain open for Kat. "Go on, we don't have much time. Try the navy dress on first. Make sure you show it to me."

Kat entered the stall. Lydia drew the curtain closed and Kat stared at all the clothes hanging around her. There were at least a dozen pieces, and more waiting for her outside the change room. Considering they didn't have much time, why was Lydia making her try on so many outfits?

She stripped down and put on the dress. It was a calf-length sleeveless dress that had very little shape. She couldn't imagine anyone looking good in it other than a runway model. She slipped out of the fitting room, tugging at the neckline of the dress self-consciously.

Lydia inspected her, frowning. "Turn around."

Kat spun around slowly, keenly aware of Lydia's eyes on her.

Lydia shook her head. "No." She picked up a pair of pants with a coordinating blouse. "Try this."

Kat returned to the fitting room and changed into the outfit. When she showed it to Lydia, Lydia just shook her head again and sent her back into the fitting room with yet another outfit.

This continued for what felt like hours—Kat trying on clothes, Lydia rejecting them. After a dozen different outfits, Kat was starting to feel like Lydia would never be satisfied with anything she was wearing.

Kat opened the fitting room curtain. This time, she didn't even make it out before Lydia shook her head.

"Take that off and try this. And these." Lydia thrust a dress at her, along with a pair of heels.

Kat took the dress from her and slipped back into the fitting room. She slid into the dress, then the pumps, a simple yet stylish pair of kitten heels. Kat never wore heels unless someone was getting married, but these were low enough to be comfortable.

Kat emerged from the fitting room and stood before Lydia. Once again, Lydia inspected her, but this time she didn't shake her head.

She took a step toward Kat, her eyes sweeping over the dress. "Hm."

She circled Kat, scrutinizing her from every angle. Kat's skin prickled, the hairs on the back of her neck standing up. It felt like Lydia was examining far more than Kat's outfit. Her eyes lingered on Kat's curves, sliding over every inch of her body.

Finally, Lydia stopped in front of her. "Take out your hair."

Kat reached behind her head and pulled her hair loose from its ponytail, shaking it out so it fell down her back. She attempted to flatten down her curls, then gave up.

She looked at Lydia, whose eyes were still on her, studying her silently. "How's this?"

"Yes, this is it." Lydia placed her hand on Kat's arm, turning her toward the mirror. "Perfection."

Kat's breath caught in her chest. Lydia's hand was still on

her arm, her touch sending electricity pulsing through Kat's body from head to toe.

She looked at herself in the mirror. The dress was a vibrant blue, and the A-line silhouette showed off her figure. It was short, but not scandalously so. The outfit was stylish and sophisticated, and it wouldn't have looked out of place on one of the women strolling around the fashion district outside.

Yet, somehow, it suited her. It was playful but mature. She never thought she'd feel comfortable in an outfit like this, yet she did.

Kat glanced at Lydia through the mirror. Their gazes met, Lydia's eyes a maelstrom of stormy grays and mesmerizing blues.

She leaned in closer, her breath caressing Kat's ear. "You look breathtaking," she whispered.

A quiver rolled through Kat's body. Although Lydia was barely touching her, she could almost feel Lydia's body against hers. She exhaled slowly, willing herself not to fall to pieces. Would Lydia catch her if she did?

"Oh! Don't you look beautiful?"

Kat turned to find the sales assistant standing nearby, that fake smile plastered on her face. Kat's face began to burn. She'd lost all awareness of everything outside of Lydia.

Lydia turned and gave the saleswoman an icy glare. "We'll take this, and the shoes. Grab your things, Kat. You can wear that out."

As she and Lydia left the boutique, Kat found her pulse racing out of control. The way Lydia had looked at her in the fitting rooms, the way she'd touched her—Kat could still feel Lydia's fingers on her skin, could hear her whispering in her ear. How was she supposed to keep herself together around Lydia for the rest of the trip?

She sighed. It was going to be a long day.

CHAPTER 6

Lydia tapped her fingers on the tabletop as she looked toward the entrance to the restaurant, irritation written all over her face. "They're late."

Kat glanced at a nearby clock. She and Lydia had arrived early, but it was now half an hour past the time the dinner meeting was due to start.

"I'm sure they'll be here soon." Lydia turned to Kat. "Once they get here, be sure to take note of anything important that comes up in conversation. You'll have to rely on your memory since you can't take notes."

Kat nodded. Lydia had said the same thing to her ten minutes ago. If this trip had taught Kat anything about Lydia, it was that she was something of a control freak. She made a mental note to never be late to anything involving Lydia.

A moment later, a waiter approached the table, addressing Lydia solemnly. "Excusez moi, madam. J'ai un message pour vous."

The waiter leaned down and spoke quietly to her. Lydia pursed her lips, her brows drawing together.

"Merci." She dismissed the waiter with a wave of her hand and let out a hard sigh. "That was a message from the owners of Belle. They've run into some kind of emergency. They're not coming."

Kat had gathered as much already. "Do you want me to call them and see if we can reschedule?"

"Yes, first thing in the morning." Lydia picked up a menu from the table. "In the meantime, I'm famished."

Kat blinked. "You still want to have dinner? Just us?"

"Of course. The food here is too good to let the reservation go to waste. Besides, it's a lovely night. We might as well enjoy it."

Lydia had a point. The high-class restaurant was far more expensive than anything Kat could ever afford. When else would she get the chance to eat at a place like this? And it was a nice night. They were seated by the window, giving them a view of the city lights stretching out as far as the eye could see. It was more of Paris than Kat had gotten to see the entire trip.

"Why don't we let loose a little?" Lydia said. "For the rest of the night, I'm not your boss, and you're not my intern. We're just two people having dinner."

Kat's stomach fluttered. Lydia seemed to have shrugged off her earlier tension, her manner relaxing slightly. But her eyes still stormed with that captivating intensity Kat found irresistible.

"Okay," Kat said. "Let's have dinner."

Lydia summoned the waiter again and spoke to him in French. Kat couldn't understand a single word.

"I ordered the set course for both of us," she explained once the waiter was gone. "It's the best way to experience the highlights of the restaurant. It includes wine pairings, but I can order something else for you to drink if you'd like."

"It's fine," Kat said. "I like wine, I just don't know much about it."

"If there's anywhere for you to start your wine education, it's in France. Good wine is abundant here."

Kat recalled their conversation on the plane. "You said you used to live in France?"

"On and off for a few years. We had a villa in the south."

"We?" Kat asked.

Lydia hesitated, just for a moment. "It's not important."

Kat frowned. Had she stumbled across a sore subject? But before either of them could change the topic, the waiter returned with a bottle of wine. He made a show of presenting it to Lydia, then poured them each a glass and stood by, waiting for Lydia to taste it.

Lydia inspected her glass, swirling it around and inhaling the scent of the crimson liquid before bringing it to her lips to sample it. She gave the waiter a nod of approval. Lydia certainly seemed to know her wines. Kat picked up her glass and sipped it slowly. The wine was even better than the champagne she'd had on the plane.

"So," Lydia said, once the waiter was gone. "Since we're off the clock now, why don't you tell me how you're really finding your internship at Mistress?" She gave Kat a firm look. "And don't give me a polite answer about how you have to start somewhere."

"I wasn't lying when I said I enjoy it," Kat said. "But it gets a little tedious sometimes."

"I'm sure it does. That will change once you move on to a permanent position."

"I just hope I can get one. The internship program is pretty competitive."

"Oh please," Lydia said. "With all the work you put in, you're guaranteed a position. And I'm not just saying that because I find your eagerness charming."

Kat took a long drink of her wine to hide her face. Every time Lydia gave her the slightest praise, it sent heat rising to her skin. Was her crush that out of control?

The waiter soon returned, serving them an appetizer, along with another glass of wine. He and Lydia exchanged a few words in French, Lydia's voice sultry and melodious. She had this enchanting way of speaking in both languages, like her tongue was caressing every syllable.

Lydia picked up one of her forks. "Bon appétit."

Kat looked down at her plate. The tiny bite-sized appetizers were unrecognizable. As Lydia began eating, Kat mirrored her, selecting a small fork and slipping one of the appetizers into her mouth. It tasted just as unfamiliar as it looked, but it was delicious, somehow sweet and savory all at once. A pleasured sound escaped from her. She clamped her hand over her mouth.

"What did I tell you?" Lydia said. "The food here is too good to miss."

As Lydia brought her fork to her mouth once more, Kat found herself staring, hypnotized by the full lushness of her lips. They were a deep crimson, almost as dark as the wine the two of them were drinking.

Kat lowered her gaze, surveying the food on her plate to distract herself. She took another bite, savoring it this time. It was heavenly. She looked around the restaurant, taking in the atmosphere. If she hadn't felt like she was in Paris before, she certainly did now.

Lydia examined her curiously. "What are you thinking?"

"Just how amazing this place is," Kat said. "And how amazing Paris is. I just wish I could see more of the city."

"Well, I know I said this trip would be all work and no play, but you might get your chance to have some fun. There are a few blank spots in our schedule, in the evenings. Perhaps I'll let you off early to go explore sometime." Lydia's voice dropped an octave. "If you're good, that is."

"I can be good." Kat bit her lip, attempting to regain control of herself. Why did she find it so hard to keep her thoughts from spilling out around Lydia?

Lydia let out an almost inaudible laugh. "I'm sure you can. Something tells me you're not capable of being anything *but* good."

Warmth crept up Kat's cheeks. Did Lydia see her as innocent? Kat didn't know why she always gave people that impression.

Apparently, Kat's indignation showed on her face.

"That's not a bad thing," Lydia said. "I find it appealing in a woman." She swirled her wine around in her glass. "Although, there's nothing wrong with being a little bad once in a while."

Kat's face grew even hotter. She took another sip of her wine. The glass was almost empty already, and it was her second. While she wasn't going to let herself get drunk, she needed a little liquid courage to get through a dinner with

Lydia. She was certain that Lydia was aware of her crush now. No, it was more than a crush. It was a sizzling, scorching flame that she was sure Lydia could feel.

Another course came and went. As they waited for the next one, Kat searched her mind for small talk.

"So, you travel a lot?" she asked.

Lydia nodded. "Mostly around Europe, but I've been all over. How about you? Have you traveled much?"

Kat shook her head. "This is the first time I've left the states. I had a trip to South America planned for later in the year, but that's not happening anymore."

"Why not?"

"I was going with my girlfriend. *Ex*-girlfriend, since she —" Kat stopped short. Lydia didn't need to know the details. "It doesn't matter. We broke up."

"I'm sorry to hear that."

"It's fine. It's in the past now. Anyway, after her, I've sworn off women forever."

"Oh?" Lydia took a sip of her wine, gazing at Kat from over the rim of her glass. "That's a real pity."

"Well, maybe not women entirely. Just relationships." The words left Kat's mouth before she realized what she was implying, to her boss of all people.

But Lydia took it in her stride. "Good for you. It's the 21st century. A young woman should feel free to explore her desires outside of a relationship."

"Exactly. I was with my ex since high school, so I've never had the chance to do that, to explore. And now, I can finally just let it all out. Go wild."

Lydia's eyebrow quirked up slightly. "You have a wild side, do you?"

"Not really, but that's the point. I want to get in touch with my wild side. Try all the things I've always wanted to do."

"Like what?"

"They're things I shouldn't be telling my boss." Kat had said too much already, and she hadn't had enough wine to blame it on that.

"Now, Kat," Lydia said sternly. "Didn't we agree that I'm not your boss for the rest of the night?" She leaned forward, studying Kat intently. "Unless you prefer it when I *am* your boss? Is that the kind of thing you like?"

At once, Kat's mind filled with all those naughty fantasies she'd had involving Lydia, setting off a flood of desire within her.

Lydia sat back, satisfaction shimmering behind her eyes. "Perhaps I was wrong about you being a good girl."

Kat's pulse quickened. How did Lydia know that that was exactly what Kat had been fantasizing about all this time?

She took a deep breath, attempting to pull herself together. Lydia was still watching her, waiting for a response.

"I don't know what I want," she said. "I've never had the chance to figure that out. I've only ever had one girlfriend before. I've only ever *kissed* one person, let alone…" She didn't know why she was admitting all this to Lydia. It was like she lost all control around the woman. "I guess what I want is to experience new things, expand my horizons. Take chances, be adventurous. Have some fun."

"I like the way you think," Lydia said. "I believe we

should all be more open about our desires." Lydia raised her glass. "To being adventurous."

She and Kat clinked their glasses together before finishing off the wine left in them. Kat was beginning to feel a pleasant buzz from it. If Lydia was affected by the wine at all, it didn't show.

"And I'm sure you'll have plenty of opportunities to gain some… experience," Lydia said. "Someone as beautiful and intelligent as you? You must have women falling over each other for you."

"I don't know about that," Kat said.

"Perhaps you need to pay more attention to the women around you."

Lydia gazed back at Kat, the suggestion in her eyes clear. It was like that moment in the boutique fitting rooms all over again. And once again, Kat found herself mesmerized by Lydia.

But before Kat could say a single word, Lydia broke her gaze and looked over Kat's shoulder. "Ah, our next course is here."

As the waiter served them, Kat's heartbeat slowed back down to normal. Their dinner continued, but Kat couldn't ignore the tension between them, or the brazen way that Lydia looked at her.

It only made Kat want her even more.

A couple of hours later Kat and Lydia returned to the hotel, having walked there from the restaurant. As they made their way up to their rooms, Kat felt light-headed and floaty in a way that had nothing to do with the wine. The food, the Parisian night sky, Lydia's very presence—it was all going straight to her head.

They reached their floor and headed down the hall, stopping in front of their rooms.

"It's late," Lydia said. "We should turn in."

Kat nodded. But she didn't move.

And neither did Lydia.

Kat's heart began to race. "So, thanks for tonight. For dinner. I had a good time."

"So did I," Lydia said. "It was certainly more enjoyable than a business meeting."

Silence lingered between them. Some invisible force seemed to hold Kat in place, binding her to Lydia.

"I…" She glanced down at her feet, hesitating. "I almost don't want this night to end."

When she looked up again, Lydia's gaze was fixed on hers, her eyes smoldering.

She took a step toward Kat. "Perhaps it doesn't have to."

Kat exhaled softly. Lydia was so close that she took over all of Kat's awareness, blocking out her sense of the world around them. Kat took a deep breath, trying in vain to calm the butterflies flitting inside her chest. Lydia's dizzying scent filled her head, perfume mixed with wine and desire.

Lydia reached out, grazing her hand up the side of Kat's arm. "We've been dancing around each other for too long."

Kat trembled, her skin tingling under Lydia's fingertips. She could feel the heat of Lydia's face next to hers, the tickle of her breath on her skin, the pull of her full, red lips, which Kat had dreamed about kissing so many times.

Those had just been daydreams. This was real. Her fantasy might become reality, if she just let go.

Lydia's hand grazed Kat's cheek. Kat closed her eyes, letting the gap between their lips grow ever smaller…

Across from them, a door slammed shut. Kat pulled away from Lydia, turning to see an oblivious housekeeper pulling a laundry cart.

The housekeeper turned toward them, startled. "Mon dieu!" She brought her hand to her chest. "I'm sorry, I didn't see you." She backed down the hall, apologizing profusely in both English and French.

Kat turned back to Lydia. She was suddenly aware that her hand was hovering an inch from Lydia's waist. She jerked it back, her head spinning. What was she doing? What was she thinking? She'd never done anything like this. She shouldn't have been doing this, not with Lydia. She couldn't do this.

Lydia's voice pulled her out of her head and back to reality. "Are you all right?"

"I'm fine," Kat said quickly. "It's just, the wine is going to my head." It was the only excuse she could think of.

Lydia stepped back abruptly. "You're right. We both had too much to drink."

Kat's stomach sank. She hadn't meant to suggest that she was drunk. "I…"

But it was too late. The moment had slipped away.

"Let's turn in for the night," Lydia said. "We have an early start tomorrow."

"Right." That was a good idea. This was all just a mistake. Kat fumbled in her purse for her room key and unlocked her door. Mumbling a goodnight to Lydia, she entered her room and shut the door behind her.

Kat leaned against the door and sank to the floor, screwing her eyes shut. She'd just been moments from kissing Lydia.

And then she'd practically run away and slammed the door in Lydia's face.

She groaned. She'd messed everything up.

CHAPTER 7

Kat followed Lydia to the elevator bay of the Belle Magazine offices. It was Thursday evening, and the meeting they'd rescheduled had just finished. Kat's head was full of figures and notes to write down later.

As far as she could tell, the meeting had gone well. She'd finally gotten to witness the dramatic business negotiations she'd imagined she'd get to see while working at Mistress. Lydia had been impressively commanding. It did nothing to stifle Kat's attraction toward her.

She held back a sigh. How had she managed to screw everything up between them?

Lydia turned to her. "Did you make a note of Belle's projected sales numbers for the next few quarters?"

"Yes," Kat replied. "I got everything."

Lydia gave her a curt nod. "Type it all up for me when we get back to the hotel, while everything is fresh."

Kat nodded. Since that night, after dinner, Lydia had returned to behaving like nothing more than Kat's boss. It was even worse than before. Lydia had pulled away completely. Kat didn't blame her. Kat had so clumsily rejected her, after all.

And the worst part? She still wanted Lydia. Badly.

But maybe this was a good thing. Hooking up with her boss was a crazy idea, for so many reasons.

The elevator arrived, empty. They entered and it began to descend with excruciating slowness. Kat couldn't think of anything more torturous than being trapped alone in this small space with Lydia, separated by only a few feet. Every moment in Lydia's presence was a moment she could crack and let all her desires for the woman spill out.

Somehow, she managed to keep her mouth shut all the way to the ground floor. They made their way out onto the street and looked around for a cab. The sooner they were back to the hotel, the sooner she could hide in her room, away from Lydia and the inescapable tension between them.

As they waited, Kat heard the clop of hooves. She looked in the direction of the sound. A carriage, pulled by two pure black, impeccably groomed horses, was making its way down the street toward them. She stared at it as it approached, stopping nearby. It was obviously just a diversion for tourists, but Kat couldn't help but wonder what it would be like to roam the streets of Paris in it, seeing all those sights of the city she longed to see.

The driver dismounted and opened the side door of the carriage, helping the passengers, a young couple, out of it.

Lydia spoke next to her, pulling her out of her reverie. "Something catch your eye?"

Kat shook her head. "I wish I could take a ride in one of those, that's all."

Lydia looked at the carriage, then back at Kat. "Why don't we hitch a ride? We don't have time for a tour of the city, but we need to get back to the hotel somehow."

"It's okay. We can just find a cab."

"Come on now. Weren't you saying the other night that you wanted to be more adventurous?"

Kat's heart skipped a beat. This was the first time Lydia had spoken a single word about that night.

"This is our last night here," Lydia said. "Let's have some fun. Be a little naughty."

Kat hesitated. While this hardly counted as adventurous, she could certainly use a little fun in her life. "Okay. Let's do it."

With her usual unwavering confidence, Lydia strode over to the carriage. By the time Kat caught up with her, Lydia was deep in conversation with the driver, who was shaking his head.

"I'm sorry, madam," he said. "I only do bookings. That was the last for the day. And I only drive a set route."

Kat's shoulders sank. So much for that.

But Lydia didn't give up. She switched to French and continued speaking to the man, gesturing toward Kat before taking her purse out of her briefcase. The man glanced at Kat, then nodded as Lydia slipped him a handful of bills. Kat still wasn't used to the look of Euro bills, but she was certain they were hundreds.

The driver stuffed them in his pocket before opening the side door of the carriage.

Lydia nodded to Kat. "Hop in. We're taking the scenic route back to the hotel."

Kat stared at Lydia, uncertain of what had passed

between her and the driver, but she didn't question it. She got into the carriage, Lydia behind her. The canopy was up to protect them from the wind, and the leather seats were soft and smelled heavenly.

The driver smiled at them and spoke briefly to Lydia in French before closing the door and taking the driver's seat.

Kat looked at Lydia, frowning. "How did you convince him to do this?"

"I simply made it worth his while," Lydia replied. "And I told him it was your first time in Paris and I wanted to show you how beautiful the city was. I may have embellished a touch."

Embellished? Before Kat could respond, the carriage jerked into motion. At once, Kat forgot about her question. She stared at the city around them as they turned onto a cobblestone laneway. The sun had almost set, and the dark sky had an orange glow. They were far from the Eiffel Tower and all the other tourist landmarks, but there was still so much to see. Beautiful buildings, people dressed stylishly, couples having romantic dinners alfresco. It was like a whole different world.

Kat turned to Lydia. "I should thank you for this. It's just incredible."

"It's the least I can do," Lydia replied. "We're going home tomorrow, and you didn't get to see much of Paris. Consider this a thank you for all your help on this trip."

"I'm just glad I got to come along with you. This entire trip has been amazing."

Kat sighed wistfully. The whole week had been a whirlwind. It was just the escape that she'd needed.

But in twenty-four hours she'd be on a plane back home to her old life.

And she'd no longer be alone with Lydia.

She turned toward Lydia once again, to find Lydia looking back at her. Kat steeled herself. She had to say something, or she'd regret it forever.

She drew in a steadying breath. "About the other night."

Lydia held up her hand. "Don't. Nothing needs to be said."

But despite the firmness in her words and manner, there was something in Lydia's eyes that betrayed her. They were filled with the same hunger they'd shown that night in front of their rooms. And once again, Kat found herself with the same urgency she'd felt that night.

But before she could say another word, the carriage ground to a halt.

Kat sat back in her seat. They'd arrived at the hotel. The driver dismounted and opened the door for them.

"Merci," Kat murmured, disembarking.

He gave her a nod. "You're welcome. Enjoy your time in our lovely city."

As Lydia got out of the carriage, the man spoke to her in French once again. Kat couldn't understand much of what they were saying, but she distinctly heard the word *amour*. Even she knew what that word meant. What was that about?

As the carriage drove off, Lydia turned to Kat. "You know what? Forget about those notes. You can type them up for me later. Take the evening off."

"Are you sure?" Kat said.

"I'm sure. I have nothing else on my schedule today except the conference call, and I don't need you for that. You wanted to see Paris, didn't you? It's still early, so now is your chance. You're free from all work obligations until tomorrow morning."

"Okay. Sure."

Lydia gave Kat a nod. "I'll leave you to it."

"Wait," Kat blurted out.

"Yes?"

Kat hesitated. "What did you tell the driver to convince him to give us a ride?"

A hint of a smile crossed Lydia's lips. "Are you sure you want to know?"

Kat nodded.

"I told him you're my lover and we're on a romantic getaway in Paris."

Kat's cheeks grew warm. "Oh."

"Does that bother you?"

Kat shook her head. "No."

Lydia looked Kat up and down, silently studying her for a moment.

"One more thing," she finally said. "I'll be done with my conference call in a couple of hours. After that, I'm completely free. If there's anything you need from me tonight, anything at all, come see me. I'll be in my room."

Kat nodded. "Okay."

But it wasn't until Lydia had walked away that Kat began to wonder if there was a hidden meaning behind her words.

∼

Lydia shut her laptop and got up from the desk, stripping off her clothes as she headed for the bathroom. It had been a long day and an even longer week. She needed to loosen up. She'd have a shower, slip into something comfortable.

Then, she would wait.

She entered the bathroom and stepped into the shower. She turned it on and let out a long, satisfied sigh as the water flowed over her bare skin, the warmth relaxing her muscles. As steam rose around her, thoughts of Kat filled her mind.

When the two of them had gotten on the plane to Paris, Lydia had resolved to maintain a professional distance from Kat. That hadn't lasted long. The night they'd had dinner together? The second Kat had taken a sip of that wine, had let her guard down? That brief, fleeting second when their lips had almost touched?

All those moments had chipped away at Lydia's resolve until none was left.

The days following had been excruciating. Kat's reaction at the end of the night clearly signaled that Lydia had been too forward. But since then, Kat had only seemed to want her even more. Lydia could feel it in the way Kat spoke to her, how she looked at her, practically pleading for Lydia to take her.

Lydia desperately wanted to do just that. But she didn't play games. There could be no uncertainty about what Kat wanted. She needed Kat to come to her.

But Lydia hadn't been able to resist giving Kat a nudge.

Lydia finished showering and dried off, then brushed the tangles out of her hair before slipping into her robe. She'd finished her conference call early, so she still had plenty of time to spare. She left the bathroom and took a seat on the couch, stretching out and grabbing some light paperwork to look over while she waited.

This was their last night in Paris. Tomorrow, she and Kat would return to the real world, to their regular roles as boss and employee. But here, far away from the reality of their lives back home, it was all too easy to throw away their inhibitions and let their desires run free.

Could they forget about the rules, just for one night? That was up to Kat.

Right on cue, there was a knock on the door. Lydia rose from her seat and answered it.

Standing in the doorway was Kat.

Their gazes locked, Kat's eyes shimmering with an irresistible combination of determination and lust.

Lydia leaned casually against the door frame. "Yes, Kat?"

"I…" Kat glanced down, as if collecting herself. But as she did, her eyes slid down Lydia's robed body, taking it in. When she looked up again, her gaze was even more full of desire than before.

Lydia knew what Kat longed for. And how she longed to give it to her. But Lydia needed her to say it. She needed Kat to ask.

"What do you want?" Lydia asked, her voice dropping low. "I need you to tell me."

Kat's lips parted ever so slightly, a soft rush of air escaping them. Lydia wanted nothing more than to kiss those lips. But still, Lydia waited, resisting the urge to pounce.

Finally, Kat spoke.

"I want to go wild."

That was it. That was all Lydia needed to hear.

Without hesitation, she drew Kat into a fiery, aching kiss.

CHAPTER 8

Kat closed her eyes, dissolving into Lydia's lips. Her whole body trembled, the heady, unyielding kiss rippling through her from head to toe. She wrapped her arms around Lydia's neck, clinging desperately, her fingers slipping through Lydia's soft, silken hair.

Their lips still locked, Lydia pulled Kat into the room and shut the door. She deepened the kiss, drawing Kat in closer, her hands on Kat's hips and her body pushing hard against Kat's. A breathless murmur rose from Kat's chest, a surge of heat flooding her.

Lydia broke away. "I've been waiting for you," she whispered, her eyes shimmering with lust. "Waiting for you to come to my door, waiting for the chance to give you what you've been craving."

Kat stared. So Lydia's words, they'd been an invitation, a siren song to lure Kat to her.

And now, she was under Lydia's spell.

"Tonight, you're going to let go of all your inhibitions. Tonight, I'm going to show you pleasures you've never experienced." Lydia grazed the back of her fingers down the side of Kat's cheek. "One night, no strings. But remember, what happens in Paris stays in Paris."

Kat nodded slowly. She didn't care about anything other than tonight. Nothing existed outside this moment, this room.

Lydia drew Kat in and kissed her again, her lips growing more deliberate, more demanding. Slender hands traveled up Kat's body urgently, sweeping over her hips, her waist, her breasts, her neck. A moan fell from Kat's lips. She ran her hand up the front of Lydia's chest, grabbing onto Lydia's shoulder to steady herself. With Lydia pressed against her, the thin, delicate silk of the woman's robe betrayed that she wore nothing underneath it. Deep in Kat's body, desire flickered and flared.

Lydia swept her toward the bed in the center of the room. She slid her hand down the front of Kat's thigh, all the way to the hem of her dress, yanking it up over Kat's head. She tossed the dress aside and took a step back, drinking in Kat's near-naked form, studying her every curve and dimple with a ravenous gaze.

She ran a hand down the center of Kat's chest. "You should know, I don't let anyone into my bed without a safeword."

A safeword? Wasn't this exactly what Kat wanted, to go wild, to be adventurous? Just the suggestion of a safeword made her pulse race. She glanced around the room in search of inspiration. Her eyes fell upon a vase of flowers on the nearby desk.

"Carnation," she said.

"Carnation it is."

Lydia pushed Kat backward gently, sending her sprawling onto the enormous bed. As Kat shifted back against the pillows, Lydia climbed onto the bed and crawled toward her, slowly. Kat's breaths grew heavier, the ache of anticipation emanating through her from deep in her center, all the way to the tips of her fingers.

Lydia trailed her fingers along Kat's shoulders, sliding the straps of her bra from them, sending a shiver along Kat's skin. Lydia reached around and unhooked Kat's bra, slipping it from her arms in one swift motion, baring Kat's breasts to the cool air.

Lydia looked down at her, speaking in a low whisper. "I thought you were perfection in that dress I bought you. I was so wrong."

A tremor went through Kat's body, her bare skin sprouting goosebumps. Lydia's gaze seemed to burn her, but she couldn't look away. Everything about Lydia was captivating. Her blue-gray eyes, so passionate and intense. Her lips, so luscious and full. The way her red robe, barely a shade brighter than her auburn hair, clung to her body. Kat yearned to pull Lydia down to her, to strip off her robe, to kiss her again, but she was paralyzed by Lydia's presence and her own overpowering need.

"So," Lydia said. "Do you really want to go wild?"

"Yes," Kat said softly. She didn't know what Lydia had in mind, but she wanted to find out.

Lydia got up from the bed and gave Kat a sharp look. "Stay."

Even if Kat was capable of disobeying her, she had no intention of going anywhere. She propped herself up on her elbows, watching as Lydia brought a leather duffel bag over to the bed. She opened it up and withdrew two items—a pair of handcuffs and a blindfold.

She held them up before Kat, one in each hand, dangling them from a finger. "Choose."

Kat glanced at the blindfold, then the handcuffs. Having sex with her boss in a Paris hotel room was crazy enough, but even Kat's fantasies hadn't been this wild. And yet, the unmistakable throbbing between her thighs told her that she wanted this just as much as she wanted Lydia.

"Well?" Lydia said. "Of course, you can choose neither. I'm perfectly capable of giving you a night of unforgettable pleasure without these."

Kat shook her head. "I'm just... deciding." She glanced between the blindfold and handcuffs, then pointed to the handcuffs. "Those."

"Good choice." Lydia tossed the blindfold into the leather bag and climbed back onto the bed. "Hands behind your back."

Kat brought her hands together behind her back. Lydia slipped the handcuffs onto Kat's wrists and fastened them closed with two audible clicks, one after the other. The cuffs weren't tight, but they felt heavy and secure. As Kat tested her bonds, she realized that the way her arms were restrained pushed her chest out in the most titillating way. Heat rose to her skin, a combination of self-consciousness and arousal.

Lydia pushed Kat back down onto the bed. "Now I can really have some fun with you."

Kat's skin prickled, the metal of the handcuffs cold against her bare back. As Lydia threw one leg over her, her knees at either side of Kat's hips, her discomfort vanished.

She gazed up at Lydia, the fire in her core swelling and raging. With Lydia on top of her, her hands restrained, she was entirely under Lydia's power. Those nerves, those doubts she'd had earlier? They were gone now.

And in their place was pure, unbridled desire.

As Kat stared up at her, Lydia untied her robe and slipped it from her shoulders, letting it slither down her body and pool on the bed beneath her in a puddle of silk. Kat had been right. Lydia had been wearing nothing underneath, and now, her body was on display for Kat, every inch of her bared unashamedly. Her auburn tresses cascaded over her shoulders, and her skin was clear and supple. Her flushed breasts had an inviting roundness to them that made Kat regret choosing the handcuffs.

Lydia looked down at her, devouring her with her eyes. "Do you have any idea how long I've wanted you for?" she asked, her voice dripping with need. "I've wanted you since the moment I first saw you, since the day you started working at Mistress." She traced her hand along Kat's collarbone and down between her breasts. "And you've been driving me crazy this entire trip. When you put on that dress in the boutique? If that saleswoman hadn't been there, I would have pulled you into the fitting room and fucked you there and then."

Kat exhaled sharply. Somehow, she managed to find her voice again. "If you want me, come and get me."

Lydia gave her a stern look, which did nothing to stifle Kat's arousal. "When you said you wanted to go wild, I didn't think I'd have to tame you. We've been working together long enough that you should know *exactly* what I expect of you."

She drew her fingers over Kat's breasts, sculpting her nipples into hard peaks with her fingertips. Kat let out a low murmur, the ache between her legs growing.

Lydia continued downward, grazing her fingers past Kat's bellybutton, over her panties and down to where her thighs met. "I expect you to be a good little pet and not talk back to me."

Kat shuddered and rose up on the bed, rocking back against the other woman's hand, trying to smother the throbbing inside her. Lydia pushed Kat's now soaked panties into her slit. Kat's eyes rolled back, her mouth opening wide in a silent cry.

"I expect you to do exactly as I say."

Lydia withdrew her hand from between Kat's thighs and tugged at the waistband of Kat's panties. Kat lifted her hips, wriggling in an attempt to help Lydia move faster. But Lydia peeled them down carefully, inch by inch, taking her sweet time.

Finally, Lydia pulled Kat's panties from her ankles and placed them to the side. She slid her hand up the entire length of Kat's leg. "I expect you to yield to me in every manner possible."

Kat's thighs parted involuntarily. She was more than willing to yield to Lydia. She would have done anything just to feel her touch, her lips, her fingers inside. She stared back at Lydia, begging silently. Underneath her back, her fingers curled, her arms straining vainly at the cuffs that bound them until the metal dug into her wrists.

Lydia ran her hand up the inside of Kat's leg, all the way up to the peak of her thighs. Kat closed her eyes and let out a long, slow breath, opening herself up to Lydia.

"Yes," Lydia said. "Yield to me."

She snaked her fingers up Kat's slit, brushing them lightly over her entrance and up to her clit. A moan slipped from her mouth, pleasure darting through her. As Lydia circled Kat's swollen bud with a fingertip, she sank into the bed, submerging herself in the torrent of heavenly sensations. The impossibly soft bedsheets beneath her. The low, rhythmic sound of Lydia's breaths. The feel of Lydia against her. Kat let it all wash over her until she was drowning in it.

Just when Kat couldn't take it anymore, Lydia slid her finger down to Kat's entrance. "Do you want me to fuck you?"

"Yes," Kat whispered. "Please."

Kat's eyes were still closed, but the way Lydia's body hitched against hers was unmistakable. "I didn't even have to tell you to beg," she said. "I always knew you were the submissive type."

Before Kat could process Lydia's words, Lydia slipped her fingers inside. Kat drew in a pleasured gasp, clutching at the bedsheets underneath her, holding on tightly as the world rocked. With every stroke of Lydia's fingers, every brush of Lydia's thumb against her clit, she came more and more undone. She ground back against Lydia, trying to match her thrusts, but it was hopeless with her arms bound.

A whimper escaped her. "Please."

"Oh?" Lydia purred. "Do you want me to let you come?"

Kat nodded, afraid that if she opened her mouth to speak again, she wouldn't be able to contain herself.

Lydia picked up the pace, stroking and delving and curling her fingers. It only took seconds for Kat's pleasure to reach a peak. Her head tipped back, and a wild cry erupted from her chest, a powerful climax tearing through her. Her entire body quaked as she rode out her orgasm, Lydia's unrelenting fingers drawing out her ecstasy.

As Kat fell into a post-orgasm haze, Lydia pulled her close, kissing her deeply. Kat murmured with bliss, arching back against her, relishing the feeling of Lydia's body on hers. Their legs intertwined as Lydia ground back against her, the heat between Lydia's thighs slick against Kat's skin.

"Can you feel how wet you make me?" Lydia asked. "Can you feel how much I want you?"

"Yes," Kat said, breathless. Without thinking, she tried to reach out and touch Lydia, but her wrists were still cuffed. "My hands," she protested.

"What do you need your hands for?" Lydia shifted to sit back against the pillows, parting her legs. "I'm sure you can figure out a way to make me come without them."

Kat skimmed her eyes down Lydia's body. Suddenly, not having the use of her hands was the last thing on her mind.

She crawled between Lydia's legs, balancing precariously on her knees, and leaned over, kissing Lydia on the lips softly. She worked her way downward, trailing her lips all over Lydia's body, letting her mouth do what her hands couldn't.

She kissed her way down Lydia's neck, inhaling her sweet perfume. She kissed her way over the gentle mounds of Lydia's breasts, letting her tongue skate over Lydia's nipples. She kissed her way down Lydia's smooth stomach, all the way to her outspread thighs.

"Yes," Lydia said, her hips rising. "Taste me."

Kat dragged her mouth down Lydia's slit, parting the

woman's lower lips with her tongue, sliding it over her folds. She was warm and wet, and smooth as silk. Kat ran her tongue up to Lydia's clit, eliciting a low moan from her. A shiver rolled through Kat's body, the sound resonating deeply.

Suppressing her arousal, she teased and strummed at Lydia's bud with her tongue. Lydia's breathing grew heavy, her breasts rising and falling. Kat pursed her lips around Lydia's clit, sucking it lightly. A whispered curse fell from the other woman's mouth.

Kat took that as a sign she was doing something right. She continued working Lydia's clit, drawing soft, fevered groans from the other woman's chest. Lydia's hands fell to Kat's head, her fingers twining through Kat's curls, holding on as her thighs began to shake. She was close. Kat could feel it.

Not a moment later, Lydia's legs locked around Kat's head, her hands gripping Kat's hair tightly and her hips shaking against Kat's mouth. As she succumbed to her orgasm, her cry echoed through the room, on and on, until finally, she fell silent.

Kat lay stretched out on the bed, her face buried in a pillow, half-tangled in sheets. As soon as Lydia had uncuffed her, she'd practically passed out.

The bed swayed under her, then she heard Lydia's footsteps receding. Groggily, she opened her eyes and looked around the room. Lydia stood by the window, pushing it open. Moonlight streamed through the window and the cool Parisian night air breezed into the room, blowing her silk robe gently.

Kat sat up. "Do you want me to go?"

Lydia turned back to her. "Of course not. I was just getting some fresh air."

Kat lay back down. "Good, because my legs don't work right now."

Lydia returned to the bed and slipped back into it. Kat let out a long, satisfied sigh.

"You know, I almost didn't come here tonight." She turned her head to face Lydia. "Did you really know I'd come?"

"I did," Lydia replied. "Although, it certainly took you long enough."

"How did you know?"

"Let's just say, I could tell how much that wild side of yours wanted to come out."

Kat glanced at the leather bag beside the bed. "Is that why you brought handcuffs with you on a business trip?"

"No. I simply like to be prepared when I travel. And I have more than just handcuffs and a blindfold in that bag of mine."

"Does that mean you do this kind of thing a lot?"

"You could say that. Although most of the time, there's no sex involved. And usually, there's far more involved than just handcuffs."

Kat studied Lydia's face. "Are you some kind of... Dominatrix?"

Lydia chuckled softly. "I'm a Domme, yes. And it seems you're not as innocent as I thought."

Kat scowled, her annoyance only half-hearted. "I never

said I was innocent." She paused. "So what, you like tying people up? You like hurting them?"

Lydia shook her head. "I don't like hurting anyone. And BDSM isn't all whips and ropes. And it's about so much more than the physical acts themselves. It's about something far deeper. You've already experienced it on some level."

Kat frowned. "What do you mean?"

"When I handcuffed you, how did it make you feel?"

Kat shrugged. "It was a turn-on, that's for sure."

"That's not what I'm talking about." Lydia reached out and took Kat's hands. "Close your eyes."

Kat shut her eyes. Lydia drew Kat's arms up, bringing them together above her head. She ran her hands up the inside of Kat's forearms, then wrapped her fingers around Kat's wrists, sending a tingle along her skin. Even after the events of the night, Lydia's touch still made her weak.

"When I handcuffed you, something changed in you," Lydia said. "I could feel it. I know you felt it too. What happened?"

As Kat tried to think through the fog of lust Lydia's touch evoked in her, understanding came over her. "I just kind of... stopped thinking. I let go of everything."

"That's right. In restraining you, I took away a small part of your power." Lydia's low, melodious voice sent a frisson through Kat's body. "It's easier to let go, of all your doubts, your thoughts, your problems, when you have no control. It's easier to give in to all your naughty little desires when you're powerless to resist them. It's easier to surrender when you have no choice. That's the pleasure of submission."

Submission. Was that what that feeling had been? When

Kat had knocked on Lydia's door, her nerves had been in overdrive, but as she'd lain, handcuffed and helpless on Lydia's bed, her mind had emptied of everything, all doubt and hesitation fading away.

And letting go had been so freeing.

"There's far more to what you can do with a pair of handcuffs—or ropes, or a blindfold—than meets the eye," Lydia said. "Tonight was just scraping the surface."

Kat chewed her lip thoughtfully. "I guess I have a lot to learn."

"It's a pity this is our last night here. There's so much I could show you. I could take you on the most incredible journey without us ever leaving the bedroom." Lydia released Kat's wrists. "But this is most definitely a one-off. As soon as we get on that plane tomorrow, it's back to business as usual. Tonight never happened."

"Right. That's probably for the best." But Kat couldn't keep the disappointment out of her voice.

"Come here."

Lydia pulled Kat in close, enveloping her with her arms. Kat curled against Lydia's chest. She would indulge in this moment of intimacy. Because as soon as they returned home, everything would go back to normal.

As soon as they left Paris tomorrow, they would leave this night behind them.

CHAPTER 9

"Lydia," Yvonne said. "Are you busy?"

"Not at all. Come in." It was Monday morning and Lydia was attempting to get through all the work that had piled up in her absence. However, she was finding it difficult to focus. Her mind was still on Paris. No, not Paris.

Kat.

Yvonne took a seat in front of Lydia's desk. "I'd like to discuss the Paris trip in more depth. We didn't get to talk about the details during the meeting this morning."

"What would you like to know?" Lydia asked.

"Let's start with the Belle Magazine meeting. It sounds like everything went well."

"That's right. Although nothing is official, the deal is in the bag. They did have some concerns about whether we'll be keeping the company's structure intact."

"That shouldn't be a problem," Yvonne said. "How did they feel about our plan to scale down print and focus on an online presence?"

"They're a little resistant, but I'm sure they'll come around."

As Yvonne continued, Lydia's mind wandered back to Paris, to the final night she and Kat had spent in the city. It had been several days since then, but Lydia hadn't been able to stop thinking about her. She was consuming Lydia's every waking thought. And when Lydia closed her eyes, her mind filled with images of Kat—at Lydia's hotel room door, working up the nerve to tell Lydia that she wanted her. On the bed, naked and pleading with Lydia to grant her release. In Lydia's arms, nestled against her in the aftermath of their passion.

Lydia shouldn't have let things between them go so far. She shouldn't have let her guard down. And she certainly shouldn't have invited Kat to her hotel room. She'd hoped that a one-night stand would get rid of all the tension between them. Instead, it had stoked the flames even further.

"How was location scouting?" Yvonne asked. "Did you find anything suitable for our Paris office?"

Lydia refocused her attention on the conversation at hand. "Most of the options weren't centrally located enough, but there are a few that could work. I'm having Kat write up a report on the top three. I'll send them to you once she's done."

She made a mental note to follow up with Kat about it later. She hadn't spoken to Kat since they'd arrived back from Paris. She'd been putting it off because she knew that if she saw Kat, she'd want her all over again.

It was unusual, how much Kat was getting under Lydia's skin. When it came to women, Lydia wasn't the type to be ruled by physical lusts, but there was something about Kat that made her want to give in to all her primal desires. Kat hadn't been the only one to let go that night. Lydia rarely let herself be that free and unbridled during sex.

Lydia's attraction to Kat was more than just physical. There had been other women since Emily that Lydia had been attracted to, but the intense pull she felt toward Kat was something else entirely.

However, they had both agreed to leave Paris in Paris. And Lydia planned to do just that.

By the time she and Yvonne were done, it was almost midday, and Lydia was starting to feel the effects of jet lag. It was nothing a cup of coffee wouldn't fix.

Yvonne rose from her seat. "I'll let you get back to work. By the way, I'm grabbing lunch with Gabrielle and Amber soon. Care to join us?"

"Maybe next time," Lydia said. "I have too much work to catch up on."

As Yvonne left the room, Lydia felt a twinge of guilt. Yvonne and the others who ran Mistress always made sure to invite Lydia along when they were spending time together outside work. Even Yvonne, who was normally quite reserved, made an effort to include her. But Lydia turned down their invitations more often than not.

It was rude of Lydia. Although she always had good reasons for declining their invitations, they were just excuses. This was yet another way she was avoiding moving on with her life. Forming new ties, new connections with people, meant she'd be well and truly settling into her new life here. It wasn't just her social life she was avoiding moving forward with. She still hadn't hired an assistant or sold her old house, and her new apartment was filled with boxes she hadn't unpacked, even though she'd moved in months ago.

It was entirely irrational. Lydia had chosen this. She'd moved halfway across the country, left everything behind, in order to start a new chapter, but every step she took away from her old life left her with the feeling she was leaving Emily behind. Emily herself had wanted this for her, for Lydia to move on after her death. Lydia had promised Emily she would do so.

However, moving on was easier said than done.

Lydia picked up her coffee mug. It was empty. She was seriously starting to regret not hiring an assistant. For now, she'd have to get her own coffee.

She rose from her desk and left her office. As she headed toward the break room, she spotted Kat sitting at her desk. An ember of desire sparked inside Lydia, but she smothered it quickly. She would have to control herself if they were going to continue to work together.

She strolled over to Kat's desk. It took a moment for Kat to notice her.

She looked up at Lydia. "Hi."

Lydia steeled herself. "Have you finished the report on the potential office locations?"

"I'm working on it right now. I'm almost done."

"Good. Send it through to me once you're ready."

Kat nodded. As silence stretched out between them, their gazes remained fixed together. Kat's eyes were always so expressive, betraying what lay behind them even when she tried to hide her feelings. And as Lydia stared back into them, she saw Kat peering up at her as she lay handcuffed in the bed in Lydia's Paris hotel room.

Come and get me.

Kat broke the silence. "Is there anything else?" Her voice was soft and pleading.

Lydia cleared her throat, collecting herself. "No," she said firmly. "That's all."

Hurt flashed in Kat's eyes. Lydia felt a tugging in her chest. Pushing the feeling aside, she turned and swept off to the break room.

When she walked by Kat's desk again on her way back to her office, Kat was nowhere to be found. As Lydia took a seat behind her desk, she couldn't help but wonder—was Kat upset? Was she struggling with the idea of leaving everything between them in Paris?

Had their decision to do so been a mistake?

Lydia shook her head. She couldn't even consider the possibility. Everything that had already happened between them was bad enough. If word got around that Lydia had slept with an intern, the board wouldn't hesitate to use it as an excuse to get rid of her.

She had to put the idea out of her mind. And if she needed to, she'd talk to Kat to make sure she understood the same. Pursuing anything further with Kat was out of the question. Not just because Kat worked for her. Not just because Lydia could lose her job.

The real problem was that Lydia wanted Kat in a way that felt deep and real. And with that in mind, getting involved with Kat wouldn't be fair to her.

Because in the end, Lydia's heart was still with Emily.

When Kat returned home from work that night, she found Meghan in the kitchen stuffing leftover boxes of takeout in the fridge.

"Hey," Meghan said. "I ordered Thai from that new place. There's plenty left if you want some."

"Sure," Kat replied. "I'm starving."

She grabbed a plate and dished out some leftovers, then stuck them in the microwave. She leaned back against the counter and let out a heavy sigh. A week ago, she'd been enjoying the finest of Parisian cuisine, and now she was eating reheated takeout.

Meghan gave her a sympathetic look. "Long day?"

Kat nodded. "The Paris trip left me with a lot of work to do."

"Speaking of which, how was the trip?" Meghan had been working most of the weekend, so they hadn't had much time to catch up since Kat got back.

"It was great. Getting away for a while was just what I needed. And Paris is so beautiful." Kat missed it already—the lights, the glamour, the romance. She couldn't stop thinking about it.

And she couldn't stop thinking about Lydia.

"So you got some time off to have a little fun in the end?" Meghan asked.

"Not really. But I did get to fly first class, and the hotel was amazing. Plus, Lydia and I had dinner at this amazing restaurant one night."

Meghan raised an eyebrow. "So, your boss, who you totally have a crush on, took you out for a fancy dinner?"

"It's not what you think," Kat said quickly. "Well, actually, it kind of is. It was a business meeting that got canceled, so we had dinner together, and there was all this wine, and we almost kissed, but then I chickened out, and then we did kiss—"

"Hold up." Meghan's mouth dropped open. "You kissed your boss?"

Kat nodded.

"Wow. I didn't think you had it in you. You've always been such a good girl."

Kat crossed her arms. Why did everyone think she was so innocent? "Actually, we did a lot more than just kiss."

"Holy shit! You had sex with Lydia?"

Kat nodded.

Meghan smirked. "Spill. I want all the dirty details."

Kat grabbed her dinner from the microwave and took a seat at the kitchen bench. As she waited for her food to cool, she filled Meghan in on what had happened between her and Lydia. She kept the details to herself, but it didn't stop Meghan's smirk from growing.

"Anyway, we both agreed that it was a one-off thing," Kat said. "And when I went into work today, Lydia was just acting like it never happened. I guess I shouldn't be surprised, but still…"

Meghan examined Kat's face. "Does that bother you?"

"I don't know. Maybe. I don't know what I expected. Just not this."

Kat's stomach churned. Was she really supposed to pretend she and Lydia hadn't spent that incredible night together, and that Lydia hadn't handcuffed her and given her a mind-blowing orgasm before teasing her with the prospect of far kinkier things?

Meghan frowned. "Are you not okay with what happened? She's your boss, after all. Do you feel like she took advantage of you?"

Kat shook her head. "Definitely not. I was the one who went to her room that night. But now I just can't stop thinking about that night. I can't stop thinking about *her*."

"Then why don't you do something about it?"

"Because Lydia made it clear that it was just a one-night stand. Anything more is too risky. And I agree with her. We work together. The last thing I want is to get involved in something so complicated."

"I guess you're right," Meghan said. "Oh well, plenty of fish in the sea."

"I'm not interested in fish. I'm done with fish forever."

Meghan rolled her eyes. "Yeah, you said that already. About a billion times."

"Because it's true."

"So what, you're just going to be alone for the rest of your life because of Brooke?"

Kat scowled. "Do we really have to have this conversation again?"

"All I'm saying is that you can't hold onto what happened with her forever."

"I'm not holding onto it. I'm completely over her."

"Sure, maybe you're over *her*, but are you over what she did?" Meghan asked. "It's eating at you, I know it is. You say you're okay, but you've become this bitter, jaded person. It isn't you."

Maybe Meghan had a point. What had happened with Brooke had shattered Kat's world. It wasn't just the cheating, or the breakup itself. It was the fact that her entire life had been ripped out from under her in the process. Since high school, Brooke had been everything Kat had known. After high school, she'd moved away from her family so she could come to college here, with Brooke. They'd lived together the entire time. And all Kat's friends, everyone she knew here in the city, were Brooke's friends too. Kat had spent almost ten years building her whole life around the two of them being together.

And it had all crumbled in a matter of seconds.

When it had, she'd had no one to turn to other than Meghan. The entire time that Brooke had been cheating, with one of their mutual friends, no less, all their friends had had their suspicions and not a single one told Kat. Had they gossiped about her, behind her back, laughing at how she couldn't see what was right in front of her face? Had they pitied her? Kat didn't know. She hadn't spoken to any of them since, especially considering most of them were still friends with her ex.

Just like that, she'd lost trust in every single person in her life.

So maybe she was a little jaded, but she had a good reason for feeling the way she did.

"Look," Kat said. "I know you're just looking out for me, but you don't need to worry about me. I'm fine."

"You say that, but you don't act like it," Meghan said. "I wish you'd just talk to me about it. You know I'm here for you."

"I know," Kat said. Meghan was the exception, the one

person in Kat's life she knew she could trust. "And I'd talk to you if there was anything to talk about. But there isn't."

Meghan gave her an exasperated look, but she dropped the subject. As Kat started on her dinner, she began daydreaming about Paris again. She'd give anything to be back in Paris instead of here, in her dreary, boring life.

But it wasn't just the escape of Paris itself that she longed for. It was the escape she'd found with Lydia that night they'd spent together. No, it had been more than an escape. When she'd been alone with Lydia in her hotel room, at Lydia's mercy, she'd felt free in a way she never had before.

How would it feel to truly submit to Lydia's will? What would it feel like to have Lydia show Kat all those things she'd alluded to as they'd lain in bed, sweaty, spent, and satisfied?

She was starting to realize her desire for Lydia was more complex than just lust. She was drawn to that dominant part of Lydia in a way that ran deeper than simple attraction.

And she couldn't ignore it any longer.

CHAPTER 10

Kat stared blankly at the copier as she waited for it to finish. She sighed. Here she was again, stuck spending her days making copies and organizing files. Right now, Paris seemed a world away.

Her thoughts were interrupted when Angela, the internship supervisor, entered the copy room. The short-haired, middle-aged woman was balancing a mountain of files in her arms.

"Good, you're still in here," she said. "Once you're done with that, I have a job for you."

"Sure, what do you need?" Kat already had enough to do, but as an intern, she didn't have the luxury of turning tasks down.

"I need you to copy these." Angela dropped the armful of files on the table next to the copier. "And file the copies once you're done."

Kat eyed the pile of files, trying not to let her lack of enthusiasm show. "Sure thing."

"If you need some help, just ask Courtney." With that,

Angela hurried from the room, no doubt to saddle some other intern with a heap of paperwork.

Kat opened the file at the top of the pile. She wouldn't be asking Courtney for help. All the interns were envious of Kat because she'd been chosen to go to Paris with the CFO of the company, but unlike the others, Courtney didn't even bother to hide her resentment. Just being around her made Kat uncomfortable.

She didn't blame any of the interns for feeling that way. The trip had been an incredible opportunity. And yet, Kat was starting to wish she'd never gone to Paris at all.

Kat loaded the first set of documents into the copier and pressed start. After a few seconds, the copier ground to a halt, an error message flashing on its screen. It had run out of paper. Kat looked around, but the shelf where the paper usually sat was empty.

She headed for the supply closet, irritation welling inside her. She was at the end of her rope. But it had little to do with her job, and everything to do with Lydia.

It had been a week since that night in Paris, and forgetting about what had happened between her and Lydia had proven impossible. Every time Kat saw her, Lydia's eyes were filled with that same fiery lust they'd had when Kat had turned up at her hotel room door. Every time Lydia spoke to her, she recalled the way Lydia's lips had tickled her cheek as she whispered into her ear. And the one time she had brushed against Lydia as they'd passed each other in the office, Kat recalled the feel of Lydia's body against hers, the caress of Lydia's fingertips on the insides of Kat's wrists as she'd cuffed them together.

It was maddening. She didn't know how much more of this she could take.

Kat reached the supply closet and shut the door behind her. She grabbed a ream of paper, along with some pens and other supplies. But instead of leaving, she closed her eyes and took a deep breath, trying desperately to settle all the building emotions. The glass walls of the office offered very little privacy, but this was one of the few rooms that had actual walls. She needed a moment to collect herself. Breaking down in front of everyone wasn't a good look for an intern.

She was still attempting to pull herself together when she heard the supply closet door open behind her. As the door clicked shut, the telltale scent of perfume filled the room. Kat turned around slowly.

Lydia.

Kat's heart skipped a beat. "I was just going," she stammered.

But she didn't move. Lydia's gaze held her in place, restraining her just as well as that pair of handcuffs had. She was powerless against the spell Lydia cast on her.

"We need to talk." Lydia took a single, measured step toward her, stopping before she got too close. "I'm sensing some... tension between us."

That was an understatement. With the two of them alone in the small space, the entire room crackled with electricity.

"This is about Paris," Lydia said.

"Yes," Kat murmured.

"What we did that night. It's made you uncomfortable around me. I never intended that."

Kat shook her head. "I'm not uncomfortable around you. That's not what this is."

Lydia examined her intently, silence simmering between them. They were separated by only a couple of feet. Kat hugged the ream of paper to her chest as if it could protect her from the heat of Lydia's gaze.

"We agreed," Lydia said. "We agreed that what happened in Paris stays there."

Kat nodded. "I know." The words spilled from her lips before she could stop them. "But maybe it doesn't have to stay in Paris."

Lydia tensed. "We can't."

"Why not?"

"You know why. You work for me."

"There aren't any rules against it. I checked."

"It's not that simple," Lydia said sternly. "If anyone finds out about us, there will be repercussions. It will put your internship at risk."

"I don't care about my internship."

"You can't honestly expect me to believe that. I know how important working here is to you."

Lydia was right, and Kat knew it. But right now, she wanted Lydia even more than she wanted a job at Mistress.

"My job is at risk too," Lydia said. "If the board found out I was involved with an intern, they wouldn't hesitate to get rid of me."

"Then we don't let anyone find out," Kat said. "We'll keep it a secret."

Lydia shook her head. "It's too risky."

"I know it's risky. But I just can't ignore the way I feel. And I know you feel the same way."

She studied Lydia's face, searching for confirmation. While the woman's expression remained hard, indecision flickered in the blues of her eyes.

"I can't go back to the way things were," Kat said. "I can't just pretend nothing happened between us. I've tried, I really have, but I can't ignore this. You awakened something in me that night. You made me feel this hunger for something I didn't even know I wanted."

Kat took a step closer to her, and another, closing the space between them until they were almost touching. Her heart thudded inside her chest. "I want this. I want to go wild. I want you to show me all those things we talked about." She looked deep into Lydia's eyes. "I want you."

The words had barely left Kat's mouth before Lydia's lips were against hers, kissing her fiercely. Kat let out a gasp, the pens and paper she was holding tumbling to the floor. Lydia backed Kat against the shelves, one hand on Kat's hip, the other sliding up the back of Kat's neck. Kat grabbed hold of the shelf behind her, her body threatening to collapse from the intensity of Lydia's kiss.

Lydia pulled away slightly. "We can't."

But she didn't let go of Kat. Instead, she kissed her even harder. Kat melted against her, seizing Lydia's shoulders to pull her impossibly closer—

Lydia drew back again. "We can't." She glanced back at the door. "Not here. Not now."

"What are you saying?" Kat searched Lydia's eyes. "We're doing this?"

Lydia let out a sigh of defeat. "Yes, we're doing this. You just know how to push all my buttons, don't you?" She reached up and traced the edge of Kat's chin with a finger.

"But this is the last time I'll let you get away with being so demanding."

Kat exhaled softly, recalling Lydia's words in the hotel room in Paris. *Do as I say. Be a good little pet. Yield to me.* When it came to taking charge, Lydia was just as unrelenting in the bedroom as she was in the boardroom, and Kat found that irresistible.

Lydia pulled away and straightened up her rumpled blouse, her controlled demeanor returning. "We'll continue this tomorrow night. I'll send you the address of a hotel. Until then, it's business as usual, do you understand? All it takes is one slip up, and we could both lose our jobs."

Kat nodded.

Lydia pulled Kat into her and kissed her again, slower, more deliberately this time. A tremor went through her. Was this a promise of what was to come? She would find out soon enough. She'd just have to wait until tomorrow night.

Lydia drew back. "We've been in here far too long. I need to go." She walked over to the door and reached for the door handle. "One last thing. About tomorrow night."

"Yes?" Kat said.

"Don't forget your safeword."

After Lydia left the room, Kat lingered in the supply room, catching her breath. She'd need to keep a level head in order to keep everything with Lydia under wraps.

One slip up. That was all it would take.

CHAPTER 11

The next evening, Kat made her way to the address Lydia had given her. The five-star hotel was almost as grandiose as the hotel they'd stayed at in Paris. She was glad she'd chosen to dress up a little, or she would have looked out of place. She wore her favorite dress, a knee-length blue number that she saved for special occasions. After all, a secret rendezvous with Lydia called for something classier than the jeans and sundresses she normally wore.

Kat entered the lobby and headed for the reception desk. Lydia had given her detailed instructions on what to do when she arrived. She was to go to the desk and give her name. A key would be waiting there for her. She was to take the key, go up to room 313, knock on the door, wait ten seconds, and open it.

What would happen after that? Only Lydia knew.

Kat greeted the receptionist and gave him her name. He handed over a keycard without a further word. If he had any idea that he was facilitating an illicit fling, it didn't show.

Kat couldn't deny the thrill it gave her. It only made her anticipation grow.

She got into the elevator and rode it up to the third floor, then made her way down the hall, checking the number at each door. 301. 303. 305. All the way to 313.

Taking a deep breath, she knocked on the door, counted to ten in her head, and unlocked it.

She entered the room. Lydia was inside, reclining on a chaise lounge at the end of the bed. Kat stared at her. Lydia always looked breathtaking in the stylish yet professional outfits she wore at work, but this was something else. The black pencil skirt she wore was shorter than her work skirts, short enough to show the tops of her thigh-high stockings and the garter belt straps holding them up. Instead of a blouse, she wore a black corset embroidered with red lace roses. It cinched in her waist, emphasizing her slender curves in the most mouth-watering way. Her hair was pulled back in its usual sleek ponytail, not a strand out of place.

"Shut the door," Lydia said. "And come in."

Kat closed the door and stepped into the room, silently awaiting Lydia's instructions.

"I trust you didn't have any trouble finding the place?"

Kat shook her head. "No."

Lydia gave her a hard look. "Tonight, you will address me as Mistress Lydia. Or simply Mistress, if you prefer."

Kat's face grew warm, both from the scolding and from Lydia's command. "Yes, Mistress." *Mistress Lydia* seemed too formal, but *Mistress* felt natural.

Lydia rose from her seat and sauntered over to where Kat stood, her hips swaying as she balanced effortlessly on stiletto heels. "That's the first thing you need to learn. Fundamentally, the relationship between a Domme and her sub is about the exchange of power, freely given, of course. How you address me reflects that. Now, do you remember your safeword?"

Kat nodded. "Carnation."

"Good. I'll let you in on a little secret. That safeword? It means that you're the one in control here. You have the power to stop everything with one little word." Lydia reached out and tipped Kat's chin up with her finger. "But until you use it, you're mine to command. You will be a good pet and do exactly as I say. You will obey my every instruction. Do you understand?"

Kat nodded, then added, "Yes, Mistress."

Lydia released Kat's chin, her lips curling in a satisfied smile. "You learn quickly. You're just the perfect little kitten, aren't you?"

A shiver went down Kat's spine. If she was a kitten, Lydia was a wolf, poised to pounce on her helpless, cornered prey.

And Kat was desperate to be devoured.

She stood in place as Lydia walked over to the bed and picked up a coil of rope from the pillow.

She began unwinding it carefully. "Take off your dress," Lydia said.

Clearly, Lydia wasn't wasting any time. Kat removed her coat and stripped off her dress, slinging both over the back of a nearby armchair. She'd put all that effort into her outfit, only for it to end up tossed aside. She folded her arms over her chest, waiting. She still had her bra and panties on, but there was a slight chill in the room.

The rope unwound, Lydia returned to where Kat stood, holding it in her hand. "Give me your hands."

Kat held her arms out in front of her. Lydia took Kat's wrists and crossed one over the other, then wound the rope around them, binding them together before securing them with a knot.

"There," Lydia said. "Now, let me take a look at you."

She took a step back and began circling Kat slowly, inspecting her from every angle. Kat's skin began to tingle, the beginnings of arousal flickering within her.

Finally, Lydia stopped in front of her. She hooked her fingers into the ropes at Kat's wrists, pulling her toward the chaise at the end of the bed. Then, she lowered herself down onto the lounge, reclining on her side with her legs stretched out.

She looked Kat up and down. "Take off your panties."

Heat welled up in Kat's core. She reached down to remove her panties before remembering that her hands were bound. She looked at Lydia, but Lydia simply crossed her arms and waited.

It was clear that Lydia wasn't going to help her out. Kat slipped her bound hands into the waistband of her panties, pushing them down at one side, then the other, inch by painstaking inch. All the while Lydia watched, the faintest hint of amusement in her eyes. Was Lydia enjoying this?

Finally, Kat slid her panties past the widest point of her hips. After that, it was just a matter of nudging them down her thighs until they fell to the floor on their own. She stepped out of them, pushing them out of the way with her foot.

Lydia took hold of the rope binding Kat's wrists and

pulled Kat closer to her, drawing her hand up the side of Kat's thigh and over the swell of her hip. Kat's skin prickled at Lydia's touch, the ache between her legs growing stronger. Lydia slid her hand inward, caressing the inside of Kat's thigh, her fingers brushing over Kat's nether lips. Kat's legs quivered, her knees threatening to give out under her. Lydia had barely even touched her, but she was already wet and throbbing. She craved more of Lydia's touch.

Instead, Lydia pulled her hand away and leaned back in the chaise. "Touch yourself for me. I want to watch."

Kat hesitated. Of all the things Lydia could ask of her, she wasn't expecting that. She was no stranger to self-pleasure, but it was something she did in private. For some reason, the idea of having Lydia watch her made her throb even more.

"Is there a problem?" Lydia asked.

Kat shook her head.

"I'm not hearing a safeword, am I?"

Kat remembered herself. "No, Mistress."

"Then do as you're told."

"Yes, Mistress." Lydia's stern words, her gaze, only made Kat hotter.

Her eyes still on Lydia, Kat slid her bound hands down the center of her stomach, lower and lower, until she reached the peak of her thighs. She slipped her hand into her slit, stroking gently. Her eyes fell closed.

"No." Lydia's voice cut through the still air. "Open your eyes. Look at me."

Kat opened her eyes and exhaled sharply, drawing her finger up to circle her clit. As she stared back into Lydia's eyes, she recalled that night in Paris, recalled how Lydia's hands and lips had felt on her skin and how her fingers had felt inside her. She remembered how freeing it had been to surrender her body to—

"Stop," Lydia said.

Kat bit back a groan as she obeyed. It had just started to feel good.

Lydia waved her hand in Kat's direction. "Kneel."

Her heart racing, Kat dropped to her knees.

Lydia gazed down at her, her eyes ablaze. "Ever since Paris, I've been dying to bring you to your knees."

Kat let out a shallow breath. She hadn't even hesitated at Lydia's command. Was she that deep under Lydia's spell that Lydia had control of her body?

Lydia rearranged herself on the chair, sitting upright with her feet on the ground. "Go on. Continue."

Looking up at Lydia, Kat sat back on her heels and spread her thighs apart. She slid her hand down into her slit again, rolling her fingers over her swollen bud. A soft moan fell from her.

"Kat. My kitten." Lydia let each word roll over her tongue. "Your name, it's the most wonderful coincidence. It suits you. You have a wild, untamed side, but like any good pet, what you really want is someone to belong to, someone to obey."

A tremor rolled through Kat's body. She resisted the urge to shut her eyes.

"That's what you're begging for every time you look at me," Lydia continued. "A Mistress who will tame you, not roughly, but with a firm, caring hand. One who both commands your obedience and rewards it generously."

Was it true, what Lydia was saying? Was that what Kat wanted? She was too consumed by desire to think clearly.

"Stop," Lydia said.

Ignoring her body's protests, Kat stilled her hands.

Lydia eased forward in her seat, pulling her skirt up around her waist. "Watching you is getting me all worked up. I'm going to need your help with that."

Kat stared shamelessly. Lydia was wearing nothing underneath her skirt other than the garter belt. Kat bit the inside of her cheek, attempting to distract herself from the ache between her thighs.

"You're going to make me come," Lydia said. "And I want you to keep touching yourself while you do. I'm enjoying watching you play with yourself. But there's a catch. You're not allowed to come until you make me come."

Seriously? Kat was already so close. How was she supposed to stop herself? But she didn't dare raise her objections with Lydia.

"Do not stop playing with yourself," Lydia said. "Do not stop pleasuring me. *Do not* come before I do. You may only come when I tell you to, do you understand?"

Kat nodded. "Yes, Mistress."

Lydia parted her long, stockinged legs. Kat scooted forward on her knees. She wasn't wasting any time. She buried herself between Lydia's thighs, drawing her mouth up the other woman's folds, teasing her all over with her tongue. A deep, rumbling moan rose from Lydia's chest, sending satisfaction rolling through Kat's body. She'd relived that night in Paris enough times in her head to remember what Lydia liked, what made her tremble and gasp, what tipped her over the edge into oblivion. And she planned to get Lydia there as quickly as possible.

Lydia slid her hand down Kat's neck, settling it on her shoulder. "Don't stop," she murmured. "And don't forget my instructions."

Kat had already forgotten. She slipped her bound hands between her legs again, touching herself as lightly as she could. She couldn't risk coming before Lydia did. As her fingers worked away, she zoned in on Lydia's clit with her mouth, her tongue sweeping and circling and strumming.

"Yes." Lydia's grip on Kat's shoulder tightened. "Just like that."

It didn't take long for Kat to bring Lydia to the edge. Within moments, Lydia's body began to quake, her thighs locking around Kat's head. She let out a long, slow groan, the forceful waves of her climax rippling through her body and into Kat's own. As Lydia rode out her orgasm, the heat in Kat's core flared, the sweet sound of Lydia's pleasure only increasing Kat's arousal.

Lydia exhaled slowly, her body slackening. She squeezed Kat's shoulder. "Stop."

Kat stilled her hand, but she couldn't stop a whimper falling from her mouth. Her knees ached faintly despite the thick carpet, her legs were numb, and she longed to stretch out her bound arms. But she was barely aware of her discomfort. It paled in comparison to her need. Her whole body was crying out for release.

She peered up at Lydia, awaiting the command to continue. Instead, Lydia cupped Kat's face in both hands and drew her up to her feet, kissing her with such force that

Kat's knees nearly buckled. The throbbing within her intensified.

Lydia broke away. "I want to finish you off myself. Would you like that?"

"Yes, Mistress," Kat said, breathless. "*Please*."

Lydia ordered Kat onto the bed before climbing onto it with her. She took Kat's wrists and pulled them upward, tying the loose ends of the rope to the headboard above. Kat's pulse pounded in her ears. This was a step up from simply having bound hands. She was tied to the bed, under the control of a woman who reveled in her helplessness. And yet, she was so incredibly turned on.

Lydia ran her hand down Kat's stomach and slipped it between her legs. Kat gasped, absorbing a dart of pleasure. Lydia drew her hand back, inspecting Kat's wetness on her fingers.

"You really are ready to come, aren't you?" Lydia glided her hands down Kat's chest, pulling the cups of Kat's bra down, and let her fingertips graze Kat's nipples. "Should I let you come now? Or should I play with you some more? Keep you on edge just a little longer?"

Kat pulled at her bonds, a low whimper spilling from her. Lydia stifled Kat's protests with her lips. Kat closed her eyes and sighed into the kiss, the thirst inside her deepening.

"I promised I'd reward you for your obedience," Lydia said. "I will. Just be patient."

Kat closed her eyes. Lydia kissed Kat down the side of her throat, then her chest, then the peak of each nipple, pursing her lips around them firmly. Kat's chest hitched, her breath deepening. As Lydia continued, kissing her way down Kat's stomach, the hunger within her became unbearable.

By the time Lydia's lips reached the apex of Kat's thighs, she felt like she was going to burst. She let out a desperate, pleading murmur.

But Lydia wouldn't be rushed. Slowly, she slipped her tongue between Kat's nether lips, skirting lightly over Kat's clit, sending a spark shooting through her. Lydia snaked her tongue down to Kat's entrance, darting and probing. Kat shuddered, her head rolling back as she gave in to all the sweet sensations.

Lydia hooked her arms around each of Kat's thighs to anchor herself, pushing Kat's legs up into the air. She ran her tongue back up to Kat's swollen nub, firmer this time. A moan tumbled from Kat's lips. She wrapped her fingers around the rope above her, gripping it tightly as she rocked back gently against Lydia's mouth. Lydia was an expert musician, playing Kat's body like a familiar instrument, reacting to Kat's every sound and movement.

Kat trembled. "Lydia..." Her pleasure was rising to critical levels. She remembered Lydia's earlier instructions. "Can I come now? Please?"

Lydia pulled away and looked up at her. "Yes. You may come."

She dipped her head between Kat's thighs again. It only took a few seconds for Kat to reach a climax. An eruption went off inside her, pleasure pulsating through every cell in her body. She convulsed on the bed, losing herself in the flood of ecstasy Lydia rained down upon her.

As her orgasm faded, Lydia kissed her way back up Kat's body, all the way to her lips. Kat purred, drunk on Lydia's scent and the taste of her own arousal on the other woman's tongue. When Lydia drew her into an embrace, Kat didn't even mind that she was still bound to the bed.

She let out a blissful sigh. "That was… whew. I'm really glad you cornered me in that supply room yesterday."

"So am I," Lydia said. "Although, the reason I cornered you was to tell you under no uncertain terms that we couldn't do this again. Yet here we are." She gave Kat a sharp look. "You have no idea how infuriatingly irresistible you are."

Kat smiled. "Sorry, Mistress."

Lydia untied Kat's wrists from the headboard, freeing her hands. As Kat stretched and flexed her arms, Lydia took the rope and began coiling it up carefully. When she was done, she grabbed a leather bag from beside the bed. It was the same leather bag she'd taken with her to Paris. Kat hadn't noticed it earlier. She'd been somewhat preoccupied.

As Lydia opened the bag and slipped the rope inside, Kat caught a glimpse of the bag's contents. All she could make out were a few more coils of rope and some leather straps.

"What else is in that bag?" Kat asked.

Lydia cocked her head to the side. "Why do you want to know?"

"I'm just curious." Kat hesitated. "Can I have a look?"

"Perhaps. If you ask nicely."

"Mistress, can I please have a look?"

"That's better." Lydia placed the bag on the bed next to Kat. "Go ahead. You can touch too, just be careful. These aren't toys."

Kat almost retorted that they were toys, but she held her tongue. She sat up, folding her legs underneath her, and riffled around in the bag, taking the items out one by one and placing them on the bed. The leather straps she'd seen earlier were a harness for a strap-on. There was a dildo to go with it, as well as some other sex toys.

There were also some kinkier items, like a pair of thick, heavy metal cuffs and a ball gag. Kat picked up some clamps on a chain. They looked like a torture device. She dropped them to the bed abruptly. Were they nipple clamps?

Lydia laughed softly. "This is just a selection of my tools. I wasn't planning to use them all on you."

Kat continued exploring the bag. She found some leather cuffs, as well as a set of butt plugs of differing sizes. She placed those aside as she spotted some kind of whip. She pulled it out of the bag. It had lots of little tails, each of them flat and wide.

Kat examined it carefully. "You said you don't like hurting people. Then what's this for?"

"It's true," Lydia said. "I'm not a sadist. I don't enjoy hurting people. But this kind of thing, it isn't really about pain."

"Then what is it about?"

"Give me the flogger and hold out your palm." Lydia held out her hand. "Trust me."

Kat handed over the flogger. Lydia grabbed hold of Kat's wrist. With her free hand, she took the flogger and drew it along Kat's palm, the tails of the whip tickling her hand.

"You see," Lydia began. "Pain is just another sensation."

She trailed the flogger up the inside of Kat's wrist and forearm. A shiver went through her.

Lydia raised the whip above Kat's forearm. "And more

often than not, it's about the anticipation rather than the feeling."

Kat held her breath, resisting the urge to flinch away. But Lydia only let the whip fall against Kat's skin lightly, feathering its tails along the inside of her arm.

"Do you see?" Lydia pressed her fingertips against the pulse point on Kat's wrist. "Your heart is beating faster already."

It was true, Kat's heart was racing. Although she trusted Lydia not to hurt her, she couldn't help the way her body reacted.

"It isn't about pain," Lydia said. "It's about anticipation. And in the heightened state that anticipation brings, pain itself can even become pleasurable. I can show you sometime if you'd like."

"I would." Kat paused. "At least, I think I would."

Lydia released Kat's wrist. "Let's call that a soft limit. A hard limit is anything you won't do under any circumstances. A soft limit is something you have reservations about but might be comfortable doing depending on the circumstances." She held up the flogger. "Is that how you feel about this?"

Kat thought for a moment. "Yeah, it is."

"All right. Just know that I will never push your limits without your consent."

Kat nodded. She hadn't realized until then that she'd needed to hear that. As much as she wanted to explore her kinky side, it was all unfamiliar territory.

"What else are you curious about?" Lydia asked. "What in this bag interests you?"

"Most of it, really. I'll try everything once." Kat wanted

to be adventurous, after all. "But definitely not the nipple clamps. Those are a hard limit." She glanced at the set of butt plugs. "And I don't know about those. I guess I've never really thought about doing that. You know, anal. It's not that I don't want to try it, it just seems kind of intimidating." She stopped short. Judging by Lydia's bemused expression, she was babbling. "Maybe I am a little curious, but I wouldn't want something like that just sprung on me. I guess that's a soft limit too."

Lydia nodded. "All right. Limit or not, I wouldn't spring something like that on you. When it comes to all things anal, slowness and care are important. We can talk about it when you're ready. In the meantime, there are plenty of other things we can explore."

"Right." Kat paused. "So, when are we going to do this again?"

"Impatient, are we?" Lydia shook her head in disapproval. "Don't forget what you agreed to, kitten. You are mine to command. I'll call upon you when I next see fit."

Kat held back a sigh. "Yes, Mistress."

"And when we go back to work, try to behave like the two of us aren't fucking, will you?"

"I'll try my best." For a moment, Kat had forgotten that this affair of theirs was a secret. She didn't want to risk them getting caught.

But seeing Lydia at work every day, pretending they were just boss and intern, wasn't going to be easy.

CHAPTER 12

Lydia hung up her phone and set it down on the coffee table by her office window. She'd just booked a flight to Chicago in the evening. It was last minute, and it meant she'd have to leave work early, but she had business to take care of back at her old house. She'd been avoiding it for far too long.

There was a knock on her office door. Lydia had left Kat a note to come and see her when she returned from her lunch break.

Kat entered Lydia's office and shut the door. "You wanted to see me?"

"Come here," Lydia said. "There's something we need to discuss."

As Kat approached, Lydia couldn't help but think about how easy it would be to draw Kat down to her and devour her right there on the couch. Or better yet, on her desk. The glass walls of the office were the only thing keeping her from doing so. For a moment, she considered dimming them so she and Kat could have some privacy, but she didn't want to arouse suspicion. When it came to Kat, she needed to keep business and pleasure separate.

It wasn't easy. She and Kat had been working closely with each other since Paris. Every time they crossed paths, Lydia wanted nothing more than to whisper all the things she wanted to do to her into her ear. Every time they were alone, even for a moment, Lydia found herself with the urge to push Kat up against the wall and kiss her like she had in the supply closet. All those coy, inviting glances that Kat kept giving her made it so much harder to control those urges.

If Lydia had any sense, she would keep her distance from Kat, at least at work. But instead, she was doing the opposite.

"So," Kat said. "What did you want to talk about?"

"I've been thinking," Lydia began. "Ever since we returned from Paris, you've been doing all the work I give you on top of your usual intern duties."

"I don't mind. I can handle it."

"I'm sure you can, but I'd prefer it if your attention wasn't split." Lydia folded one leg over the other, leaning back in her seat and looking up at Kat. "Besides, I want you all to myself."

Kat's cheeks flushed pink. A smile pulled at Lydia's lips. It was ridiculous, how easy it was to provoke Kat.

She continued. "I spoke with your supervisor and requested that you be assigned exclusively to me. Angela graciously agreed to let me have you. As of Monday, you'll be acting as my assistant until further notice."

It was a logical decision. Since the Paris trip, Kat had essentially taken on the role of Lydia's assistant. Whenever

Lydia needed something, she went straight to Kat instead of the other interns. Kat had access to Lydia's email, her contacts, her calendar, and she was responsible for much of Lydia's daily administrative work.

"You'll still be an intern officially, but I'll be the only person giving you tasks to do. That means no more fetching coffee, unless it's for me."

Kat smiled. "That sounds great."

"I'll make sure you're assigned a desk closer to my office. It'll be waiting for you on Monday." Lydia folded her hands in her lap. "That's all. You may go."

Kat nodded. But she didn't leave.

"Is there something else?" Lydia asked.

"Well, I was just thinking," Kat said. "It's the weekend, and I noticed you don't have anything on your schedule. Not that I was looking," she added quickly. "Anyway, I don't have much going on either. My roommate is dragging me to this party on Saturday night, but that's it." She curled a stray ringlet of her hair around her finger. "So, I was hoping we could do something together? You know, like the other night."

"Oh?" Lydia folded her arms across her chest. "So you enjoyed yourself the other night?"

Kat glanced around, as if afraid of being overheard. "I did. I haven't been able to stop thinking about it."

"You think I haven't noticed?" Lydia asked. "I can feel how much you want me every time we're in the same room."

Kat's blush deepened. She was such a contradiction sometimes. It was hard to believe this bashful woman was the same person Lydia had tied to the bed as she begged for her release. Both those sides of Kat were utterly irresistible.

"But you're forgetting one thing," Lydia said. "I told you I would call upon you when I needed you, didn't I?"

Kat lowered her head. "Yes, but…"

"Then be a good kitten and wait until I do."

Kat's shoulders sank. "All right."

The disappointment in Kat's voice was hard to miss. Perhaps Lydia was being too harsh. After all, Kat wasn't accustomed to the kind of strict power games Lydia liked to play. Lydia could string her along in the bedroom, but she had to be a lot more careful outside of it, or Kat would end up hurt.

"Look," Lydia said. "I would love to spend time with you this weekend, but I have plans. I'll be out of state." She hesitated. "I'm flying out to Chicago. I have to take care of some business. It was last minute, so I haven't put it in my calendar yet."

"Oh." Kat perked up a little. "That's okay."

"We'll get a chance to spend time together soon." Lydia lowered her voice. "Perhaps we'll go back to that hotel room and play with some of the things in my bag."

Kat glanced away shyly, hiding the smile that danced on her lips. "I'd like that, Mistress."

She left Lydia's office, a slight spring in her step. Lydia returned to her desk, determined to finish off her work so she could leave early. She had a long weekend ahead of her. She was returning home, to the house she and Emily had shared for over a decade. She'd put it up for sale months ago, and today her realtor had informed her that someone had made an offer too good to turn down.

But Lydia hadn't accepted it yet. She needed to return home one last time, to work out if she was truly ready to say goodbye, both to her old house and to her old life.

It was late when Lydia arrived at the house. The flight to Chicago, combined with the drive from the airport in her rental car, had taken some time. The house was miles outside of the city on a vast, secluded piece of land. In the past, Lydia had preferred the peace and quiet of the countryside, but over time she'd grown to enjoy city life.

She unlocked the front door and entered the house. It was less of a house and more of a mansion, sprawling, ancient, and grand. Now, the manor was empty of everything other than furniture, antiques that were going up for sale with the house. Lydia hadn't wanted to keep any of it. It clashed with her new, modern apartment, and she'd wanted to start fresh.

As she strolled through the house, memories came back to her. She passed the hall table and saw Emily standing there, admiring a vase of flowers Lydia had picked from the garden. In the kitchen, she saw Emily attempting to cook them dinner, oblivious to Lydia watching her to make sure it didn't end in disaster. As she passed the lounge room, she saw Emily sitting by the fire, so deep in a book that she didn't hear Lydia walk in.

But those memories were fainter than they used to be. Was Lydia forgetting Emily? That wasn't what she wanted. She wanted to move on, not to forget.

She felt a twinge of guilt. Things were changing in ways

she hadn't anticipated. And as she stood in the hall, she realized the house no longer held that comfortable familiarity it used to. It no longer felt like home.

But her new apartment didn't feel like home either.

Now wasn't the time to dwell on that. Lydia had plenty to do. To start with, she needed to clear the last of her things from the house. Most of it was already gone, but there were still some odds and ends left. This was the last of the loose ends she had to deal with when it came to her old life.

She grabbed a pair of scissors from a drawer in the kitchen and made her way to her bedroom. She'd stashed half a dozen boxes and suitcases in the walk-in closet there. Lydia entered the closet and grabbed an old suitcase that was sitting in the corner. She unzipped it to find an assortment of clothing and accessories. Only a few of the items inside were worth keeping, including a nice pair of leather gloves and a vintage red briefcase that she'd thought she'd lost years ago.

She tackled the boxes next, working through them quickly. Most of them contained random items, nothing worth keeping. But as she sorted through the final box, she spotted something at the bottom—a large silver jewelry box.

Lydia's heart stopped. She dug the box out and carried it carefully back into her bedroom, then sat on her bed and opened it up on her lap.

Inside was a collection of mementos of her relationship with Emily. Photos of the two of them. Gifts they'd given each other. Those little notes Emily had left everywhere for her. Emily herself had made up the box before her death. She'd given it to Lydia as a kind of security blanket for after she was gone. Lydia had sorely needed it at first, but over time, she'd stopped using it so much.

The guilt swirling in her stomach grew stronger. It had been months since she'd moved, and she hadn't even noticed the box was missing.

She reached into the box and took out a photo. It was of herself and Emily at their wedding five years ago. They'd been together for more than a decade before that, living a happy life together here in the paradise that was their mansion, leaving only for vacations or when Lydia took consulting jobs.

But their life together had been cut short. Soon after their wedding, Emily had gotten sick.

Everyone had told Lydia that knowing Emily's death was coming would make it easier. She'd have time to prepare. Emily herself had tried to prepare Lydia for it, which was typical of her. She'd always been the strong one, the one who had held them together.

But it hadn't helped. Emily's death had still crushed her.

In the aftermath, Lydia had hardened herself. It was the only way for her to get through the days without drowning in grief. Over time, her grief had faded into the steady, ever-present background noise of existence, but she'd still carried it with her.

For three long years, she'd continued to live that way, too paralyzed with grief, too afraid of abandoning Emily to move on with her life. But there had come a point at which Lydia had realized that she couldn't live that way forever. As long as she lived here, in the house they'd shared, surrounded by the constant memory of Emily and the life they'd built together, she'd never be able to move on. So, she'd decided to leave it all behind.

It was what Emily had wanted for her, after all. She had said as much to Lydia in her last days. *Don't bury yourself with me.* Those had been her words.

Lydia was finally beginning to fulfill that promise she'd made to Emily, yet she couldn't help but feel like she was betraying her by moving on.

She put the wedding photo aside and took the rest of the photos out of the box. Underneath were a few pieces of jewelry they'd exchanged, including their wedding rings. But there was one piece of jewelry that was just as precious as those rings. It bound them to each other just as strongly. It was a thick black collar made of soft leather and silver.

She picked the collar up and ran it through her fingers. Emily had been more to Lydia than just her wife. They belonged to each other in every sense of the word. That was why, after Emily's death, Lydia had turned to BDSM as an escape. She'd let her Domme persona take over entirely, drawing strength from it to cope with her grief and helplessness.

But all the women she'd been with since then, the submissives, were just a way to distract herself from the pain she'd felt. She hadn't been with them in the same way she'd been with Emily, in that real, meaningful way. Would Lydia ever be able to have that again?

But the person Lydia had been with Emily was so different from who she was now. She couldn't go back to that. But perhaps she could be with someone in a meaningful, but different way.

Perhaps someone like Kat?

Lydia returned the collar and the photos to the box and shut the lid. It was wrong of her to even consider the idea. Lydia would just end up hurting her.

Because in the end, Lydia would never be able to give Kat her whole heart.

CHAPTER 13

Meghan handed Kat a drink and joined her on the couch. "So, was I right?" she yelled over the music. "Are you having fun?"

Kat looked around the crowded lounge room. She barely knew anyone at the housewarming party other than the couple who were hosting it. They were friends of Meghan's who Kat had met once or twice. Meghan had brought her along as a guest in an attempt to get her out of the house.

And Kat had to admit, she was having a good time.

"Fine, you were right," she said. "This is kind of fun." She'd started to forget what that felt like. If things with Lydia had taught her anything, it was that getting out of her comfort zone was worth it.

Meghan grinned. "See? This is so much better than sitting around at home by yourself."

Kat took a sip of her drink and screwed up her face. It was some kind of wine spritzer. It tasted awful. All she could think about was how much better the wine she'd had in Paris with Lydia was.

She sighed. She couldn't go five minutes without thinking about Lydia. Kat was addicted to her. What would happen next time Lydia called on her? What kind of erotic games would their next encounter bring? That was assuming Lydia didn't just keep her hanging forever. After their conversation on Friday, that seemed like a real possibility.

What was Lydia up to right now, "taking care of business" in Chicago? Kat hadn't even known that Lydia had lived in Chicago. Kat knew very little about her. They rarely discussed anything personal. Lydia was a mystery to her. Was that just part of Lydia's nature, or was there something more? Were there secrets she was hiding?

Kat pushed the thought aside. She had no reason to think Lydia was keeping secrets from her. Besides, even if she was, it wasn't like Kat was entitled to know Lydia's secrets. Lydia was still Kat's boss. The two of them were just having a secret fling, that was all.

Meghan nudged Kat's arm with her elbow. "That woman in the corner? The short-haired femme? In case you haven't noticed, she's been eying you all night."

Kat didn't even bother looking at the woman. "I'm not interested." To Meghan's credit, they'd been at the party for almost two hours, and this was the first time Meghan had tried to set Kat up. Usually, it didn't take that long.

"How about someone else?" Meghan looked around the room. "Pretty much everyone at this party is queer. You have plenty of options."

"Did you bring me here to have fun, or did you bring me here to try to get me to hook up with someone?"

Meghan shrugged. "Why not both?"

"Even if I was interested, I already have too much on my plate in that department."

"Right. All that kinky sex you're having with your boss must be keeping you busy."

Kat shushed her. "That's supposed to be a secret! And that's the last time I tell you any details about my sex life."

"I'm just teasing you," Meghan said. "So is your thing with Lydia an actual thing, or is it just something casual?"

"It's definitely the latter. She's my boss, and she's way older than me. Plus, I'm pretty sure she's insanely rich. Like, billionaire rich. She's out of my league."

"Don't sell yourself short," Meghan said. "Any woman would be lucky to have you. Besides, that's all the more reason you should go for it. She's rich, hot, and she obviously knows how to keep you satisfied in bed. Why wouldn't you want to lock that down?"

Kat rolled her eyes. But maybe Meghan had a point. Although Kat's feelings toward Lydia had started as a silly crush, over time they had developed into a deeper attraction. Sure, Kat barely knew anything about Lydia's personal life, but the more time they spent together, the more she learned about who Lydia was as a person. She knew how Lydia liked things done. She knew what pleased Lydia, and what annoyed her. She knew that although Lydia was commanding and firm, she had a gentler side, a sensitivity only ever revealed in the aftermath of passion. She knew all of Lydia's darkest desires, and Kat herself shared them.

She shook her head. "I don't…"

Out of the corner of her eye, Kat spotted a pair of women standing out in the hall. Her eyes narrowed. Kat didn't recognize one of them, but the other, a tall blonde with shoulder-length hair, was someone Kat knew very well.

Brooke.

Kat's stomach iced over. She hadn't seen Brooke since the moment she'd discovered her then-girlfriend in bed with another woman. Kat had walked away without a word, turning her back on Brooke and the relationship forever.

But now, faced with Brooke once more, all the feelings Kat had felt that day brimmed up again. Anger. Resentment. Betrayal.

"Kat?" Meghan frowned at her. "What's wrong?"

Kat's heart hammered against her ribcage. She needed to get out of here.

Meghan's eyes followed Kat's. "Oh, shit. What's she doing here? She wasn't invited, I checked."

Kat tore her gaze away from Brooke. "I don't know, and I don't care." She grabbed her purse and stood up. "I'm leaving."

"Kat, wait!" Meghan grabbed her arm. "Don't go. You said you were having fun."

Kat shook her off. "I can't have fun when she's here. I'm going home."

"Okay, I'll come with you."

"No. Stay. I don't want you to ruin your night."

"It's fine, I don't mind."

Kat shook her head. "I just want to be alone."

Before Meghan could protest, Kat said goodbye and skirted around the crowd in the living room, making a beeline for the door. As she reached the hall, she saw that Brooke and the other woman were still standing there, talking to the party's hosts.

With zero hesitation, Kat fixed her eyes on the door and marched straight past them.

As she left the party, she heard Brooke calling her name.

∼

When Kat got home, she dragged herself into her bedroom and stripped off her dress, defeated. To think, she'd actually been enjoying herself.

It had been inevitable that she'd run into Brooke eventually. It was like all the lesbians in the city knew each other. Ever since the breakup, Kat had tried her hardest to avoid ever having to see Brooke again. She'd moved out of their shared apartment, blocked Brooke's number, blocked her from her life. Brooke had tried to get in touch with her in other ways, even turning up at Meghan's apartment looking for Kat, but Meghan had scared her off. Eventually, Brooke had stopped seeking her out.

And now, by total coincidence, their paths were crossing again.

Kat flopped down onto her bed. She couldn't continue like this, avoiding Brooke forever. She had a bad habit of never actually dealing with her problems, instead just ignoring them until they went away. But sometimes, her problems didn't go away by themselves. Sometimes they just festered, growing bigger and bigger until they consumed her, like right now.

She took a few deep breaths, cooling her head. Although she'd told Meghan to stay at the party, she wished Meghan was here with her. She needed a friend. And after everything with Brooke, Meghan was the only real friend Kat had left.

She pulled out her phone and began scrolling through it absently. Maybe she could find someone else to talk to. She opened her messages. Right at the top, underneath her conversation with Meghan, was her message chain with Lydia. Everything in it was work-related, mostly to do with tasks Lydia had asked Kat to do. They'd only ever discussed the other, more forbidden, side of their relationship in person.

Was it a bad idea, breaking this unspoken rule? Probably. But for whatever reason, Kat felt like Lydia was exactly who she needed right now.

She sat up and typed out a message.

Hi Lydia. Are you busy? Her finger hovered over the send button for a few seconds before she pressed it.

Lydia's reply came quickly. *No. Is everything all right?*

Kat sighed. Of course she would only contact Lydia if there was some kind of emergency, especially considering how late at night it was. Maybe this was a mistake.

Everything is fine, she wrote back. *Don't worry about it.*

She tossed her phone aside and lay back down, staring at the ceiling. What was she thinking, messaging Lydia? She didn't even know what she wanted from her.

A few seconds later, Kat's phone began to buzz, not once, but continuously.

Lydia was calling her.

Her stomach flipped. The ringing didn't stop. For a moment, she considered ignoring it, but she couldn't possibly ignore Lydia.

She picked up the phone. "Hi, Lydia."

Lydia's smooth, firm voice came over the line. "Kat, is everything okay?"

"Yeah. Like I said, I'm fine. It's nothing."

"Now kitten," Lydia said, her tone scolding. "You reached out to me for a reason. What's going on?"

"It's nothing, really." Kat hesitated. "I guess I just wanted someone to talk to. My plans for the night kind of went south."

"Oh? What happened?"

"I went to a party with my roommate, and then my ex-girlfriend showed up."

"Are you all right?"

"I'm okay," Kat said. "I just wasn't expecting to see her tonight. I haven't talked to her since we broke up, and that was months ago. Things ended pretty badly between us."

"I can see why it would be difficult, running into her like that."

"I don't know why seeing her got to me so much. Maybe it's because I never really got any closure there. The whole situation was just too messy for that to happen." But Kat didn't want to dwell on that now. "Anyway, how are things going in Chicago?"

There was a pause at the other end of the line. "A little tough, actually," Lydia finally said. "I'm at my old house, preparing it for sale. It's difficult, saying goodbye."

The weariness in Lydia's voice gave Kat pause. Lydia had never opened up to her in the slightest before. Kat could certainly relate to the feeling of struggling to move on from the past.

"Did you live there for long?" she asked.

"Almost twenty years," Lydia replied.

"Wow. It must have been hard, leaving after all that time."

"It was, but it was a step I needed to take. I wanted a fresh start. Besides, it isn't the house I'm attached to, just the memories. I've never felt the need to stay in one place for too long. It's why I like to travel." Lydia's voice took on a wistful timbre. "I grew up in a small town in Illinois. I've had this sense of wanderlust for as long as I can remember."

"Me too. I spent my whole childhood wishing I could see the world."

"Where did you grow up?"

"Oregon. We moved around the state a bit when I was a kid, but I never got the chance to leave until college. That's how I ended up moving here. My ex and I got into the same college and we wanted to stay together. But considering how things turned out, basing my life decisions on staying with my high school girlfriend wasn't the best idea." Kat sighed. "I'm sorry, I'm being a downer."

"No, you're not," Lydia scolded. "You called to talk. I'm here to listen."

"Honestly, I'm okay. I'm just disappointed that my night was ruined. I was looking forward to having a little fun."

"What can I do to help, kitten?"

Kat thought for a moment. "Well, I could use a distraction." She glanced around her dimly lit bedroom. "I'm all alone right now, at home, just lying here in bed."

"Oh? So you want your Mistress to entertain you?" The disapproval was clear in Lydia's voice. "There you go again, trying to control the terms of our arrangement, trying to get me to serve you."

This again? Kat was finding it hard to keep up with

Lydia's unwritten rules. The woman was so confusing sometimes.

"If this kind of behavior continues, I'm going to have to punish you," Lydia said.

Punish her? Kat frowned. Despite Lydia's words, there was no real irritation in her voice.

Kat hesitated. "How would you punish me?"

"Oh, where to begin? To start with, I'd have to spank you."

Kat's mouth opened in a silent gasp. The idea of Lydia spanking her like a disobedient brat was so absurd. So why did the thought make her so hot?

But Lydia wasn't finished.

"I'd spank you over my desk," she continued. "And I'd have the entire office watch."

Kat felt a thrill go through her. "But wouldn't that give away our secret?"

"You're right. Instead, I'd take you into the supply closet, where no one could see us, and I'd spank you in there. But first, I'd take off your panties and gag you so no one could hear you cry out."

Warmth prickled over Kat's skin, Lydia's words forming a vivid image in her mind.

"After spanking you, I'd have you walk around the office with no panties on for the rest of the day. And then, before you went home, I'd take you into my office, tie you to my desk, and show you who's boss."

Kat's breath hitched, eliciting an almost imperceptible laugh from Lydia.

"You'd like that, wouldn't you?" she said. "Is the idea turning you on?"

"I…" Kat's instinct was to deny such twisted desires, but this was Lydia she was talking to. Besides, she couldn't lie to Lydia. "Yes."

"Good. Because it's getting late, and I need to go to sleep so I can catch my flight in the morning. But after I hang up, I want you to think about me, while you're lying in your bed, all alone. Think about all the things I'm going to do to you as soon as I get my hands on you."

That was one command of Lydia's that Kat would have no trouble following. "And when will that be exactly, Mistress?"

Lydia tutted. "You're testing my patience, pet. And don't think I haven't noticed that you only ever call me 'Mistress' when you want something."

"Sorry, Mistress." Kat hadn't been doing that on purpose.

Lydia chuckled. "As much as I'm enjoying talking to you, I need to go. You should get some sleep too. You'll feel better in the morning."

"I'm already feeling better." Right now, Kat's problems were the last thing on her mind.

"One more thing," Lydia said. "There's something I need you to do for me."

"Sure. Anything."

"Wear something nice for me underneath your clothes to work on Monday." Lydia paused. "No, every day next week."

"Okay. I can do that." Did that mean Lydia was planning to remove Kat's clothes at some point during the week? Kat didn't dare ask.

"I'll see you on Monday. Sweet dreams."

Kat hung up the phone and sprawled out on her bed.

After her conversation with Lydia, her dreams were going to be anything but sweet.

She smiled to herself. Talking to Lydia had definitely helped. Was it strange that Kat found comfort in the roles they were playing? She liked the way that being Lydia's submissive made her feel—free and unburdened. And she liked the way *Lydia* made her feel—safe, secure, comforted. Every time Lydia called her *kitten* in that deep, sultry voice of hers, it warmed her up inside just as much as it turned her on. There was a sweetness to these erotic power games of theirs that was entirely unexpected.

But Kat had to be careful about letting her feelings run away on her. Running into Brooke tonight had been a reminder of how easy it was to end up with a broken heart.

CHAPTER 14

Lydia stopped in front of Kat's desk and handed her a file. "This needs to go to accounts. And I need that budget report from you by the end of the day, so you'll have to stay back until you've finished it."

Kat gazed up at Lydia from under her eyelashes, the thirst in her eyes barely hidden. "Sure, whatever you need."

Lydia raised an eyebrow. They were lucky no one else was around, because Kat wasn't doing a very good job of hiding the fact that the two of them were sleeping together. On the surface, her behavior hadn't changed, but the way Kat would look at her, speak to her—like she was consciously holding herself back from throwing herself at Lydia and begging her for a kiss—made it obvious that something was going on between them.

But that was Lydia's fault. She'd been toying with Kat all week, finding excuses to be alone with her so she could whisper all kinds of dirty things to her. She hadn't intended to tease Kat for quite this long, but Kat's flustered reactions were so satisfying.

Lydia planned to stop stringing Kat along soon, but Kat didn't have to know that yet.

"Is there anything else?" Kat asked sweetly.

"No," Lydia replied. "That's all, *kitten.*"

Kat's lips parted, a soft puff of air escaping them. But Lydia didn't give her a chance to respond. Instead, she turned and swept off to her office.

As she took a seat behind her desk, she couldn't help but sneak a look at Kat. Since Kat had moved desks, Lydia could see her from her office. She was working away diligently, twisting a stray curl around her finger as she did, oblivious to Lydia watching her. Sweet, shy Kat, who had gone from confessing to Lydia that she'd only ever kissed one person to calling Lydia "Mistress" in the space of a few weeks.

It was gratifying, watching Kat slowly embrace her submissive side. How Lydia longed to explore that side of Kat more deeply, to introduce her to even more of the sensual pleasures that came with submission. And she planned to do just that, when Kat was ready.

Lydia was usually a much firmer Mistress, but with Kat, she was happy to be patient. Something about her brought out Lydia's soft side. Then again, Lydia had always had a soft side. It had only been in recent years that her stony exterior had developed.

Through the glass, Kat's eyes met Lydia's. She gave Lydia a small smile, then returned to her work. Lydia smiled to herself. She was finding that she liked having Kat near, and not just in a professional sense. She felt a sense of possessiveness toward her, a need to keep her close.

That need had come to the forefront after she had

spoken to Kat on the phone that weekend. She'd been surprised that Kat had reached out to her, but she'd been glad to hear her voice. Lydia's weekend had been difficult. Although she still hadn't accepted the offer on the house, it was only a matter of time before she did. Finalizing everything with the house, knowing that she was about to walk out that door for the last time—it had brought up a storm of emotions within her. Speaking with Kat had been a welcome distraction. No, it had been more than that. It had been comforting.

At the same time, talking to Kat that night, it had awakened an intensely protective part of her that she hadn't known existed. Although she didn't know what had happened between Kat and her ex, the way Kat spoke about her, or rather, avoided speaking about her, gave Lydia the sense that Kat harbored deep wounds from the relationship. Lydia found herself wanting nothing more than to fix those wounds.

Were she and Kat crossing a line, letting things between them go beyond just sex?

And would it be so bad if they were?

I need a green marker. Find one and bring it to me.

Kat frowned. The message was from Lydia. Was she really asking Kat to find and hand-deliver a single marker to her? What was with all the unusual, tedious instructions Lydia was giving her? First that report, and now this?

Lydia had said on Saturday night that she was going to

show Kat who was boss. Kat hadn't expected that she'd meant it this way.

She sighed and got up from her desk, heading through the office. It was late evening, so there was almost no one around, not even the most eager of interns. That was a relief. Now that Kat was working as Lydia's assistant, the other interns' envy toward her had only gotten worse. While most of them were still nice, there were a few who openly resented her. Kat had to admit, it was starting to rankle.

She reached the supply closet and began hunting around. She didn't even know where the markers were, let alone green ones. Lydia seemed to be tormenting her in more ways than one. For the entire week, she'd been behaving like nothing other than Kat's boss, only occasionally letting her professionalism slip to torture Kat in the most delightfully perverse ways. Kat had spent the entire week fantasizing about Lydia doing all the things she'd threatened to do to her on the phone.

And Kat had done what Lydia had asked, wearing the sexiest bras and panties she owned every day this week. She didn't exactly own much lingerie. She was going to run out soon. Not to mention, she was going mad with lust.

She reached down to the bottom of a shelf and opened a box at random. Black markers. Hopefully, she was getting closer. As she opened another box, she heard footsteps behind her. She turned—

"Don't turn around."

Kat froze, her pulse spiking. She straightened up and turned back to the shelf. Behind her, the door clicked shut.

Then, Kat heard the click of heels, coming closer and closer, the sweet scent of Lydia's trademark perfume growing stronger.

Lydia stopped behind her. "I finally have you alone."

At once, it clicked in Kat's mind. "You don't really need a marker, do you?"

Lydia chuckled softly. "It took you long enough to figure it out. I don't need that report tonight either. What I needed was for you to stay back late, until everyone else was gone. What I needed was to get you in one of the few places in this office that we can have some privacy."

Lydia took a step closer, then another, until Kat could feel the heat radiating from her. She spoke softly into Kat's ear. "What I need is you."

Kat shivered, Lydia's velvet-smooth voice tickling her neck. Suddenly, all her irritation toward Lydia was gone.

"I told you I was going to show you who's boss," Lydia said. "And I intend to do that."

Kat let out a sharp breath, need welling inside her. She kept her head down, resisting the urge to turn and look at Lydia. The urge grew even stronger when she heard the faint swish of clothing behind her.

"Turn around," Lydia said. "Just your head."

Kat peered over her shoulder. Lydia stood behind her, her skirt pulled up around her waist, the top of her pantyhose pulled down just enough to expose the sleek black strap-on dildo jutting out from her panties.

Lydia took the pliable dildo in her hand, adjusting it so it stuck out horizontally. "You have no idea how long I've been wearing this, just waiting for the opportunity to use it."

Kat's mouth fell open. "Have you been wearing that all day?"

A smile crossed Lydia's lips. "Perhaps."

How had Kat not noticed? She'd spent half her workday staring at Lydia's body while fantasizing about her. How had Lydia hidden *that* underneath her skirt? Although she was familiar with the idea of packing, she'd never given it much thought, but she suddenly found it extremely hot.

"Perhaps I've been wearing it all week, just waiting for the right time to take you," Lydia said. "The anticipation is half the fun, after all."

"Maybe for you," Kat mumbled.

Lydia narrowed her eyes. "You should know by now that I don't tolerate bratty behavior. Are you forgetting your place?"

Kat tried her best to look contrite. "No, Mistress. It's just that I've wanted this all week."

"I know. I've been watching you getting more and more worked up, and I've savored every moment of it. I find your arousal just as delicious as your pleasure." Lydia traced the backs of her fingers down the side of Kat's throat, causing goosebumps to sprout on the back of her neck. "Perhaps I should draw this out even longer. Perhaps I should make you stand there and watch, all hot and bothered and unfulfilled, while I play with myself. Is that what you want, kitten?"

"No, Mistress," Kat said.

"Make no mistake. I want you just as much as you want me, maybe even more." Lydia leaned in closer, her full, supple lips less than an inch from Kat's. "But more than anything else, I want your submission."

Lydia pressed her lips against Kat's in a firm, insistent kiss, stealing the air from her lungs. She trembled, the ache between her legs growing. Lydia pressed her body against Kat's, the strap-on rubbing against Kat's ass cheek through her skirt, setting off sparks within her.

Lydia slid her hand down Kat's side, from her waist to her hip, all the way to the hem of her skirt. "Turn back around."

Kat turned back to the shelf obediently. Lydia pulled Kat's skirt up around her waist, exposing her bare legs and panties.

"I see you followed my instructions." Lydia drew her hand up the back of Kat's thigh and over her panties, murmuring with approval. "Aren't these pretty? It makes it all the more enjoyable for me to take these off you."

Skimming her fingers up to Kat's waist, she pulled Kat's panties down her hips and to the ground. Goosebumps sprouted on Kat's skin, the air cool on her bare thighs and ass. But inside, she burned hot.

Lydia slipped her fingers into Kat's slit from behind. "You're already so wet." She slid a finger to Kat's entrance, dipping lightly inside. "Is this for me? Is this because you've been thinking about me for days, waiting for me to fuck you again?"

Kat's whole body quivered at Lydia's feather-light touch. "Yes, Mistress."

"I've been waiting for this too. You don't have to wait any longer." Lydia grabbed hold of Kat's hip firmly. "Bend over."

Kat bent forward and leaned against the shelf in front of her, her ass sticking out suggestively. Her eyes still fixed ahead of her, she felt the tip of the dildo pressing at her entrance. She closed her eyes, anticipation swelling as she waited for her Mistress to finally give her what she wanted.

Lydia entered Kat slowly, filling her completely. Her fingers curled on the shelf before her as she bit back a moan. After being teased by Lydia for so long, just the feel of her inside was enough to send Kat's pleasure skyrocketing.

Lydia took hold of Kat's waist with both hands and began easing in and out in measured strokes. She picked up the pace, driving deeper, hitting Kat's inner sweet spot. Unable to contain herself, a moan slipped from her lips.

Lydia cut her off with a slap on her ass cheek. "Quiet now. As much as I love all those sweet sounds you make, we don't want anyone to hear us."

Kat sucked in a breath. Although Lydia's slap had been barely more than a swat, the sting on her ass cheek seemed to amplify the heat in her core. Was this what Lydia had meant, about pain and pleasure? The idea was starting to intrigue her.

As Lydia continued, pumping back and forth, she slid her hand up Kat's back and shoulders, gripping onto the side of her neck. Kat shuddered, her spine arching, every movement Lydia made jolting Kat's entire body. She reached back blindly, grabbing Lydia's hip to steady herself as her pleasure began to rise.

"Lydia," she whispered in warning. "Mistress!"

Kat covered her mouth with her hand, just in time. A muffled cry erupted from her as a deep, earthshaking orgasm rocked her entire body. Lydia thrust inside her steadily, stretching Kat's climax on and on, not relenting until Kat's head fell limply to the shelf before her.

Kat leaned heavily against it, panting hard. Lydia didn't give her a chance to recover. She turned Kat around and drew her close, draping her arms over Kat's shoulders.

"Do you have anything to say to me for finally giving you what you need?" Lydia asked.

"Thank you, Mistress." Kat could barely speak between breaths.

Lydia smiled. "Good, you're learning."

She pressed her lips to Kat's in a slow, greedy kiss. Kat murmured drunkenly, her legs threatening to collapse. If Lydia continued kissing her like this, she'd end up just as worked up as she'd been half an hour ago.

Finally, Lydia broke away. "We should get out of here."

Kat didn't protest. As she straightened out her clothes, Lydia expertly rearranged the strap-on, tucking it away in her pantyhose, then restored her blouse and skirt to their previously unruffled condition. There was no sign that Lydia still wore the strap-on, not unless Kat looked closely. There was something thrilling about sharing this secret piece of knowledge with Lydia.

When Lydia was done, she picked up Kat's panties, dangling them from a finger. "I have half a mind to keep these."

Kat's face began to burn. She was *not* walking around the office without her panties. "Can I have them back? Please, Mistress?"

Lydia seemed to think for a moment. "It is a little cold out there. I wouldn't want you to freeze on the way home."

She tossed the panties to Kat. "You can have them back. This time."

Kat muttered a thank you and slipped her panties back on. As Kat smoothed down her hair, Lydia reached out and swiped her hand along the lower edge of Kat's lip.

"Lipstick." She looked Kat up and down, then tucked a strand of hair behind her ear. "That's better. And don't worry about the report. You can go home. You leave first, just in case anyone is watching."

Kat nodded. As she made to leave, Lydia grabbed her arm, pulling her back to her.

"Just so you know, I noticed how much you liked it when I spanked you," she said. "Next time, I'm going to give you more than a spanking."

Before Kat could react, Lydia drew her in for one last, long, deep kiss, gave her a firm slap on the ass cheek, and pushed her out the door.

She blew out a breath and glanced around. The coast was clear. As she headed back to her desk and began packing up for the night, her imagination swam with Lydia's promises of "next time." What would their next secret rendezvous bring? Was Kat finally ready to dive deeper into the world of kink with Lydia, to have Lydia show her all about how pain could bring pleasure? Kat was well and truly addicted to Lydia's erotic games now, to the escape they provided.

But was it the escape that she was addicted to, or was it Lydia herself?

Kat was so lost in thought that she almost didn't notice someone standing in front of her desk.

"Courtney," Kat said. "You scared me. I didn't know you

were still here." She'd been certain all the interns had gone home.

"I thought I'd stay back and get some extra work done," Courtney said. "You know how it is. You have to work hard to get noticed around here." She crossed her arms. "And you? What are you doing here so late?"

"I'm just finishing up some work for Lydia."

Courtney's gaze flicked in the direction of the supply closet. "Is that what you were doing?"

Kat's heart skipped a beat. Did Courtney know something? Kat tried her hardest to keep a straight face. "What do you mean?"

"I'm just saying, you and Lydia seem very—" Courtney paused as if trying to find the right word. "Cozy."

"Well, yeah. I'm basically her assistant. I'm just doing my job."

Courtney studied Kat with narrowed eyes. Kat held her gaze. Could Courtney tell that she was lying? One thing was certain. The longer she let Courtney interrogate her, the more likely it was that she would slip up.

"Is there something you want?" Kat asked. "I need to finish up and get home."

"No." Courtney gave her one last sweeping look. "That's all."

Kat watched as Courtney walked away. This was *not* good.

As Kat finished packing up her desk, she spotted Lydia returning to her office from the supply room. She glanced at Courtney. Courtney was watching Lydia too, her dark eyes screwed up with suspicion.

Kat's stomach swirled. Even if Courtney was onto them,

she had no evidence that there was anything between Kat and Lydia. Kat would have to be careful not to give her any. Both Kat's internship and Lydia's job were on the line.

If anyone found out about them, there would be consequences.

CHAPTER 15

Lydia stretched out in her leather chair, watching the sunset out her office window. It was the end of the week, and she was looking forward to some downtime. Her only plans for the weekend involved unpacking the last of the boxes in her apartment. She was getting tired of all the clutter.

She looked out toward Kat's desk. Kat was long gone already. Lydia considered sending her a message to arrange to spend time together over the weekend. She could book a hotel room for them again. Perhaps they could even stay the night. They could sleep in, order room service, stay in bed all day and check out late.

It was unlike Lydia to want something like that, to wake up with another woman in her bed. She'd never felt that way with any of the women she'd been with since Emily. But Kat wasn't just any woman. When Lydia was with her, she felt more alive than she had in years.

Guilt nagged at her. She needed to tell Kat about Emily at some point. Fling or not, she and Kat were growing closer. It was starting to feel wrong, keeping something so significant from her. And the longer she put it off, the harder it became.

However, Lydia found it hard to talk about Emily with anyone. She'd become so accustomed to keeping everything buried deep inside, never letting herself be vulnerable. She'd feared that speaking about Emily, even saying her name out loud, would bring all her grief to the forefront again and she wouldn't be able to contain it. While her days of being ruled by grief were gone, it was hard to let go of old habits.

"Lydia. Good, you're still here."

Lydia looked up to find Yvonne sauntering into her office. "What do you need?"

"Madison came back from her honeymoon this morning," Yvonne said. "We're all going out to dinner tonight to catch up. Are you coming?"

Lydia reached for an excuse before stopping herself. She had no real reason to turn the invitation down. Why not have a little fun? "All right. I need a few minutes to finish up."

Yvonne nodded. "I'll meet you by the front desk." She turned and left the room.

Lydia packed up her things and made her way to the front of the office, joining Yvonne by the elevators. They made their way down to the lobby and headed for a nearby restaurant, chatting about work as they walked.

"I received word from the director of Belle Magazine this afternoon," Yvonne said. "They've agreed to our terms for the acquisition. Now it's just a matter of getting all the paperwork together and signing on the dotted line."

"That's good to hear," Lydia said.

"While we're on the topic, we need someone to act as our liaison with them during the transition. How do you feel about being that someone?"

"Sure. I'm happy to take the lead on this."

"It will require you to travel to Paris quite a bit over the coming months."

"That's not a problem. I don't mind travel. And I feel right at home in Paris."

"It will certainly be an advantage to have someone with local knowledge working with Belle," Yvonne said. "It sounds like you've spent a lot of time in Paris."

"I have. I lived in France, on and off, for a while." Lydia paused. "My late wife's family was French. We had a villa there, in the south."

Yvonne gave her a small, polite smile. "That sounds lovely."

If Yvonne was surprised that Lydia had once been married, she didn't show it. Despite having worked at Mistress for months now, even longer if her consulting work was taken into account, Lydia hadn't spoken of Emily to any of her colleagues. The weight off her shoulders was tangible.

"How is your wife doing?" Lydia asked.

"She's well," Yvonne said. "She's coming to dinner, so you'll see her soon."

They made small talk as they continued to the restaurant. Lydia couldn't remember the last time she'd made idle conversation with anyone. She'd become so withdrawn following Emily's death. And like most married couples, Lydia and Emily's social lives had been so intertwined that when Lydia had spent time with their friends after Emily had passed, she couldn't help but feel the void left by Emily. On top of that, she'd simply felt guilty for enjoying herself in the wake of Emily's death.

But perhaps it was time for her to start living again.

They reached their destination, a high-end Italian restaurant that was popular with the executives who worked in the Mistress building. Madison and her new wife Blair were already there, along with Yvonne's wife Ruby.

As they exchanged greetings and took their seats, Ruby slid her arm into Yvonne's.

"Madison and Blair were telling me all about their honeymoon," Ruby said.

"We went to the Greek islands," Blair said. "It was so secluded and peaceful. It was beautiful."

Ruby let out a wistful sigh. "That sounds so romantic." She turned to Yvonne. "I wish we'd gotten to go on a honeymoon."

Yvonne folded her arms across her chest. "This isn't the first time you've said that. It's almost like you're trying to suggest something."

Ruby flicked her blonde hair over her shoulders. "Maybe I am."

"All right, I get the hint," Yvonne said. "So then, if we were to go on a honeymoon, where would you want to go?"

Ruby shrugged. "Nowhere specific. Just somewhere warm, I think." She gazed lovingly at Yvonne. "I don't care where we go, as long as we're together."

Across from them, Blair squealed with delight. "You two are so cute. I'm so glad you ended up together. I always thought you were perfect for each other."

Yvonne smiled. "I'm glad we did too."

She leaned over and kissed Ruby affectionately. It was strange to see Yvonne doting over her wife when she was usually so reserved. Although Lydia had noticed Yvonne's demeanor had become softer over time, even at work. Was that Ruby's doing?

"If the two of you keep that up, they're going to kick us out of the restaurant."

Lydia turned to see a blonde woman standing by, her hands on her hips, looking at Yvonne and Ruby with one eyebrow raised. The woman was Amber Pryce, heiress to the Pryce family fortune. Not only was she responsible for a large part of Mistress's funding, but she was also the head of the company's non-profit wing. She didn't spend much time in the office, so Lydia didn't see her often. Her job mostly seemed to involve choosing charitable causes to throw money at and holding elaborate fundraising galas.

After greeting everyone, Amber took a seat next to Lydia. "Thank god you're here. I'm getting tired of being surrounded by all these couples. Now that everybody is married, love is all anyone can talk about."

Amber continued to drone on, barely giving Lydia a chance to speak. Lydia could certainly see the woman's perspective. With two pairs of newlyweds, there had been a lot of romance in the air at Mistress.

Amber let out an exasperated sigh. "I swear, if I have to hear the story of how Madison and Blair met one more time…"

Across the table, Blair crossed her arms. "We're not that bad. And we don't tell the story that often."

"Oh please, last time we went to dinner, you told the waiter."

Before Blair could retort, she was interrupted by the arrival of two more women, both in their early thirties. Gabrielle, a pretty, pale brunette who was Mistress's CMO, and her girlfriend Dana, a tall Black woman who was equally beautiful and had an unmistakable air of self-assuredness. Together, they were a stunning pair.

They sat down across from Lydia. Gabrielle smiled at her.

"Lydia, you came." Her surprise was clear in her voice. "You've met Dana, haven't you?"

Lydia nodded. "At Madison's wedding." Dana seemed to be the complete opposite in personality to Gabrielle. She was far more serious and aloof than her girlfriend. "Good to see you again."

Dana gave her a polite nod. "Likewise. Have we ordered yet?"

"What's the hurry?" Amber asked.

"We have a date later," Dana replied.

"Oh?" Amber said. "And who's the poor woman the two of you are trying to coax into your bedroom this time?"

Gabrielle scowled at her, but there was a playfulness in her eyes. "You make it sound so predatory. There's almost no coaxing involved. It isn't hard to find a woman who's intrigued by the idea of dating both of us. It's twice the fun."

Amber scoffed. "And twice the drama."

"Jealousy isn't a good look on you, Amber."

As Amber and Gabrielle's friendly bickering continued, Lydia tuned them out, turning her attention to Blair.

"You know, I haven't heard the story of how you and Madison met," she said. "How did it happen?"

Blair beamed. "It was a couple of years ago. Actually, everything started long before that."

As Blair began describing her first meeting with Madison in great detail, Lydia couldn't help but smile. Unlike Amber, she didn't mind all the talk of love. The happiness of all the couples was contagious. And unexpectedly, she found herself with a longing to feel that again.

What would it feel like, to experience love again, with someone new?

As Blair finished off her story, Madison cleared her throat. "Can I have everyone's attention?"

Silence fell over the table. All eyes focused on Madison.

"Now, I'm not back at work until Monday, but there's some Mistress business I want to discuss." She turned to Yvonne. "Firstly, thank you for running everything while I've been away."

Yvonne gave her a small nod. "It's no problem."

"Secondly, Yvonne tells me that Belle Magazine has agreed to the acquisition. They were very impressed with our proposal, and we have Lydia to thank for that. So thank you, Lydia, for all your hard work."

"It was nothing." But Lydia had to admit, it was satisfying to be part of a team, to build something with others. Having lived a solitary life for so long, she'd forgotten what that felt like.

"This brings us one step closer to Mistress Paris," Madison continued. "It will take some time to finalize the Belle deal, but if all goes well, this will be the beginning of something big for us. A new chapter. Of course, we still have to deal with the board, but we—"

Blair nudged Madison in the ribs. "Remember what we

agreed? No work talk until Monday. We're still on vacation."

Madison smiled at her. "All right. I just wanted to thank you all for your support. And Lydia, I'm so glad you decided to join us at Mistress, and here tonight. Now, let's order."

By the time Lydia got home, it was late, but she was feeling invigorated. She'd had a good time at dinner. She couldn't think of the last time she'd done something like that, going out for a meal just for fun, spent time sitting around talking with friends.

Perhaps putting down roots, making connections, wasn't such a daunting prospect after all.

She went into her bedroom and sat on the edge of her bed, kicking off her heels and letting out a contented sigh. Was this what moving on looked like? A few hours spent with friends? A whole day passing without her grief returning to the forefront of her mind?

A part of herself shared with someone new?

Lydia took her phone and dialed Kat's number.

She answered after several rings. "Lydia. Hi."

"Did I wake you?" Lydia asked.

"No, I'm just getting ready for bed." Kat paused. "Is everything okay?"

"Everything is fine. Are you free on Saturday night?"

"Yes." Kat's excitement was clear in her voice. "I'm completely free."

"Good. I want to take you somewhere."

"You mean, on a—" Kat stopped short. "You mean, out? In public?"

"Is that a problem?"

"No, I just thought we were supposed to be keeping things under wraps."

"We are, and we will be. Trust me." Lydia already had an idea in mind. "So that's a yes?"

"Yes, of course."

"Then I'll pick you up tomorrow night. Goodnight, kitten."

Lydia hung up the phone. She was already formulating a plan for Saturday. She wanted to do something special with Kat. More and more, she was finding herself wanting to make Kat happy, to spoil her, to dote on her.

Was she playing at romance with Kat? Was it selfish of her to do so when things between them couldn't ever go any further?

But now wasn't the time for doubt. She had to keep moving forward.

She dialed another number—her realtor's.

It took him a dozen rings to answer. His voice was groggy, and she'd obviously woken him up, but she needed to do this now. Besides, she was sure he wouldn't mind when he found out he'd finally be getting the extremely large commission he'd been waiting for.

She cut to the chase. "It's Lydia Davenport. The offer on the house? I'll take it. Let's close the deal."

After some back and forth, he promised Lydia he would inform the buyer first thing in the morning. Lydia thanked him, then hung up the phone.

As she rose from the bed and began preparing to turn in

for the night, she caught sight of the silver jewelry box on her dresser. It was the box with all of Emily's keepsakes that she'd brought back with her from her old house. She felt that familiar, nagging sense of guilt, but it was fainter than it used to be.

She was moving forward now. Taking small steps.

And on Saturday night, she'd take another step with Kat too.

CHAPTER 16

Kat awoke on Saturday morning and leapt out of bed, energized. Her good mood probably had to do with the fact that she and Lydia had plans that night. She couldn't wait.

She left her room and wandered into the kitchen in search of breakfast. She found Meghan sitting at the kitchen bench, a steaming cup of coffee in her hand.

"Good morning," Kat said.

Meghan looked her up and down. "Someone's perky today."

"It's the weekend. And I have plans."

"Let me guess." Meghan put on a sultry voice. "With *Lydia*?"

Kat shrugged. "Maybe."

"So what's the plan this time? Are you going to meet her at a hotel in secret again?"

"Actually, no." Kat grabbed a mug from the cupboard and helped herself to some coffee. "We're going out."

"Oh? You mean, on a date?"

"It's not like that." But hadn't Kat thought the same thing when Lydia had called her? Despite everything, the idea excited Kat. It was so hard not to get swept up in everything with Lydia. *So much for swearing off women forever.*

"Whatever you have to tell yourself," Meghan said. "I'm just glad you've stopped moping around the house all the time. It's good to see you happy again."

A smile pulled at Kat's lips. "I guess I am happy." For the first time in months, she was starting to feel like the future was something she had to look forward to. She couldn't help but wonder—did that future have Lydia in it?

"I almost forgot," Meghan said. "You have a package. It was delivered this morning."

"A package?" Kat wasn't expecting anything.

"Yup, and it looks like it's something fancy. It was hand-delivered and everything. It's on the coffee table."

Kat abandoned her coffee and headed into the living room. Sure enough, there was a package sitting on the table, a large white gift box wrapped with a black velvet bow.

Butterflies flitted in her stomach. She untied the bow and lifted the lid of the box. Right at the top was a small card. Kat opened it up.

To my kitten,

Wear this tonight.

The note wasn't signed, but it was obviously from Lydia. Kat recognized her elegant, flowing handwriting. Plus, no one else called her "kitten."

She sat down on the couch and placed the box in her lap, peeling back the layers of tissue paper. Underneath was an elaborate half face mask. She took it out of the box and examined it closely. Black lace accented the ivory-colored mask, and the top edge formed the slight shape of cat ears.

It was beautiful.

Meghan sauntered into the living room, munching on some toast. "So, that's what was in the box?" She took a seat next to Kat, peering at the mask. "Who's it from?"

"Lydia, I think," Kat replied.

"And why did she send you a mask?"

"I have no idea." Kat placed the mask down carefully on the table before her. "There's more."

As she pulled more tissue paper out of the box, it occurred to her that its contents might be something meant for Kat's eyes only. She wouldn't put it past Lydia to have sent her something risqué. She glanced at Meghan, but Meghan's attention was on the mask, so she pulled back the rest of the tissue paper.

Her mouth fell open. Underneath was a short black cocktail dress with long sleeves and a plunging neckline, made of layers of sheer, floaty fabric.

"What is it?" Meghan asked.

Kat lifted the dress out of the box. It was the dress she'd been admiring in the boutique in Paris that day. Now, Paris seemed like a lifetime ago.

"Wow. Talk about hot." Meghan looked at the tag, apparently recognizing the label. "Not to mention pricey. Lydia gave this to you?"

Kat nodded. "And she wants me to wear it tonight."

"Where are the two of you going on this date of yours?"

"No idea. Lydia just said she'd pick me up."

Meghan grinned. "I like this woman. She sure knows how to keep a girl in suspense."

Kat sighed. "You don't know the half of it."

Lydia waited in the backseat of the car in front of Kat's apartment, the leather bag at her feet. Kat was due out any minute now. Lydia couldn't wait to see her in that little black dress. For once, she intended for both of them to remain clothed, at least for the first part of the night.

Finally, Kat emerged from her building. As she started toward the street, Lydia exited the car. Kat spotted her and hurried over, hugging her coat around her.

"Sorry I'm late," she said. "I was trying to fix my hair."

"It's all right," Lydia replied. "Did you bring the mask?"

Kat nodded. "And I'm wearing the dress."

"Good. I want to see it."

Kat glanced around, then removed her coat, revealing the black cocktail dress from the boutique in Paris. Lydia slid her eyes down Kat's body. The dress fit her perfectly, the light fabric clinging to her curves in the most tempting manner.

"I was right," Lydia said. "That does look stunning on you."

Kat murmured a thank you, a coy smile on her face. For a second, Lydia battled the impulse to pull Kat into the car and take her dress off right there in the backseat.

But she resisted the urge, waving Kat into the backseat of the car instead. "Let's get going."

Lydia slid into the seat next to Kat and shut the door. The partition between the front and back seats was up so that they could have some privacy. As the driver pulled the car out from the curb, Kat turned to Lydia.

"I love this dress, by the way," she said. "I'm surprised you remembered."

"Of course I did," Lydia replied. "I'm glad you like it. I want my kitten to be happy."

"I am. Thank you."

Kat hesitated, then leaned over, pressing her lips to Lydia's softly. Lydia felt a surge of lust. Kat had this way of kissing her, sweet and teasing, like she was inviting Lydia to devour her.

But it was far too early in the night for that.

Lydia broke away. "We need to get ready."

"Ready for what, exactly?" Kat asked. "Where are we going?"

Lydia shook her head. "You'll find out when we get there."

Kat frowned, but she didn't protest.

"Don't pout at me like that." Lydia cupped Kat's cheek in her hand. "Trust me, you're going to enjoy this. I'm taking you somewhere special. Somewhere we can truly explore that wild side of yours." She released Kat's cheek and picked up her leather bag, placing it in her lap. "Now, put on your mask."

Ever the obedient submissive, Kat produced her mask from her purse and slipped it over her head. It covered the entire top two-thirds of her face, leaving only her nose and mouth free. Lydia took her own mask out of her bag, an elegant black eye mask with ivory lace trim. It was twin to Kat's, the colors reversed, but it only covered her eyes and it didn't have ears.

"So, why the masks?" Kat asked.

"They're a disguise of sorts," Lydia said.

"You mean, in case anyone sees us together?"

"Yes, and no. Where we're going, discretion is sacrosanct, so it won't matter if anyone sees us. While these masks will help keep prying eyes away, they're not only meant to hide our identities. They're a symbol, something to signal to the world that we're not us for the night. And where we're going, masks are commonplace, whether you can see them or not."

Kat's brows drew together in thought, but she didn't question Lydia any further.

"One last thing." Lydia riffled through her bag and took out a velvet pouch. "Give me your hands."

Kat held her arms out before her. From the pouch, Lydia produced two bracelets, wide cuffs made up of several rows of pure white pearls, accented with silver. Each had a tiny silver padlock as a clasp.

Lydia fastened the bracelets around Kat's wrists. "These cuffs may look pretty, but they're sturdy enough to do the job."

As Kat inspected the cuffs around her wrists, Lydia reached into her bag again and withdrew two silver chains, one long and one short, both the thickness of a finger. She took the shorter chain and used it to clip Kat's wrist cuffs together. The length of the chain meant that Kat could stretch her wrists to shoulder-width apart, but no farther. Lydia attached the second chain to the center of the first one. The free end of the chain formed a handle, which she held onto like a leash.

Kat examined her bonds, a ghost of a smile playing on

her lips. Lydia knew that face, that blissful, faraway look stemming from all the intoxicating feelings that came with submission. She knew those feelings intimately. If she'd had any doubts about how deep Kat's submissive desires ran, she didn't anymore.

"You look beautiful." Lydia took Kat's hand, drawing her fingers over the cuff around her wrist. "A collar would have been more suitable, but that's something of a commitment. Earning one takes time."

Unexpectedly, Lydia found herself wondering—would she and Kat ever get to that point, where Lydia would consider collaring her, binding Kat to her in such an intimate way?

It wasn't long before the car pulled to a stop. She glanced out the tinted window. "We're here."

The driver got out and opened up the passenger door. As Kat slid out of the car, Lydia draped Kat's coat over her shoulders. Kat tucked her cuffed hands close to her body, hiding them from view. She needn't have bothered. It only took a few steps before they were at their destination.

Lilith's Den.

She ushered Kat through the door and into the lobby. The doorwoman greeted Lydia by name. While Lydia was a member of the exclusive club, Kat was a guest, so she was given the usual waivers to sign.

As Kat finished off the paperwork, Lydia removed her coat, revealing the corset she wore underneath. Immediately, Kat's gaze was drawn to her, a hungry look in her eyes.

Lydia held back a smile. Kat was anything but subtle.

How no one had caught onto this secret relationship of theirs was a mystery.

Lydia held out her arms. "Your coat."

Kat's hands were bound, so Lydia helped her draw the coat from her shoulders, handing them over to be checked in along with her bag.

"I have a room upstairs booked," Lydia said. "Have my bag taken up."

The doorwoman nodded. "Sure thing."

Lydia turned to Kat and took a step back, inspecting her one final time. "Wait. Take out your hair."

Obediently, Kat reached up and freed her hair from its bun, which was no easy feat with her hands bound to each other. As she shook her hair out, Lydia arranged it to fall over Kat's shoulders.

"That's better," Lydia said. "It suits you. And it completes your disguise." She tugged on the leash, pulling Kat closer to her. "Tonight, you're not Kat. You don't work for me. I'm not your boss. I am your Mistress, and you're my treasured pet. Do you understand?"

Kat nodded. "Yes, Mistress."

"Let's go inside. Stay close to me." With another tug of the leash, Lydia drew her toward the door and into Lilith's Den.

CHAPTER 17

As Lydia led her through the darkened club, Kat tried her hardest not to stare. She could count the number of times she'd been to a regular nightclub on one hand, but Lilith's Den was something else entirely. Not only was it far more luxurious than any club she'd ever been to, but it was obvious from the crowd that people didn't come to Lilith's Den simply to drink and mingle.

Lydia had been right about one thing—she and Kat blended in with their masks. There were plenty of other people wearing them, and even those who weren't wearing masks were dressed in unconventional outfits, from cocktail wear, to latex, to leather.

Lydia pulled Kat toward a corner at the back of the room, cordoned off with a sheer curtain. Lydia drew the curtain back, revealing a cozy den of plush chairs with cushions scattered all over the floor. She pulled on the leash, drawing Kat toward the chairs, and took a seat, crossing one leg over the other. As Kat moved to sit next to her, Lydia shook her head.

"No pets on the furniture," she said.

Kat frowned. Did Lydia expect her to just stand there?

Lydia picked up a nearby cushion and placed it on the floor next to her feet. "Sit."

Kat glanced down at the cushion. Lydia wasn't kidding about Kat being her "kitten" for the night. Why did the idea make her so hot?

She lowered herself onto the cushion, tucking her legs underneath her. She glanced around self-consciously, but no one was looking at them. A Mistress and her "pet" were nothing unusual here.

She settled back on her heels, her cuffed hands in her lap. Lydia's hand fell to Kat's head. She ran her fingers through Kat's hair gently. Kat felt a shiver of warmth go through her.

"So," Lydia said. "What do you think of this place?"

Kat looked out at the club beyond the curtain. "It's... a lot to take in. But I like it."

Lydia smiled. "I thought you might. I wanted to bring you somewhere you could embrace your submissive side without fear of judgment. That's what places like this are all about. Although, I had selfish motivations for bringing you here too. I wanted to show you my world. This is where I most feel at home."

Kat understood why Lydia would feel comfortable here. The club was a beautiful, eclectic tapestry, a mix of glamour, elegance, and kink. Kat could see the appeal. However, she was a little taken aback by the brazen displays of sexuality going on in the club. From her seat on the floor, she could see a half-naked woman being tied to some kind of rack contraption in front of a casually watching audience.

Although Kat had become far more adventurous recently, she still preferred to keep some things behind closed doors.

Lydia seemed to read Kat's mind. "As tempting as it is to tie you up in front of everyone, we're keeping a low profile tonight. There are rooms upstairs, private rooms, designed for all kinds of activities." She let her voice drop low. "But there's a specific activity I have in mind. Remember when I told you I could show you all about pain and pleasure, about sensation? I want to do that with you tonight, if you're ready."

"I… I'd like that," Kat said. "I think."

"You think? I need you to be sure."

Kat nodded. "I'm sure." She'd been thinking about it, but she hadn't had the chance to bring it up with Lydia yet.

Lydia reached down and touched Kat's cheek. "Don't worry, I'll take care of you."

Kat hadn't realized until then that she'd been a little tense since they'd entered the club. Lydia's words, her touch, they sent all that tension dissipating from her.

"The room won't be ready for a while," Lydia said. "Until then, we'll have to wait down here. Have a drink and relax."

As if on cue, a waitress appeared with two glasses of champagne. With a nod to Lydia, she placed them on the table before disappearing again.

"Here." Lydia handed Kat one of the glasses, careful to ensure Kat had a secure grip despite her chained hands.

It hadn't escaped Kat's notice that Lydia liked to restrain Kat's hands at every opportunity. At first, she'd thought that Lydia simply enjoyed having Kat helpless, at her mercy. While that was definitely true, Lydia seemed to like that it made Kat dependent on her, made Kat *need* her, even more.

Lydia liked having a pet to command as well as praise, someone to lavish with luxuries like jeweled cuffs and pretty dresses, someone who would sit gratefully at her feet. And Kat was more than happy to be that someone.

Kat took a deep drink of her champagne, savoring it slowly. She rearranged her legs, letting them lie to the side, and leaned against Lydia's legs. She could get used to this. As she and Lydia talked, she took in the atmosphere of the club. Nearby, a woman was wearing a leather hood that covered her entire face except for her eyes, along with a skintight leather catsuit.

Was the woman wearing a costume, or was it the other way around? Perhaps all these people were all expressing their true selves, which they suppressed in the outside world. It certainly seemed like that with Lydia. And it was beginning to feel like that for Kat too. There was something freeing about it, about kneeling at her Mistress's feet. She loved the escape that came with submitting to Lydia, the feeling of release that came with it. As Lydia's kitten, Kat didn't have to worry about a thing.

"Are you still with me, kitten?" Lydia asked. "You drifted off for a minute there."

Kat looked up at her. "Sorry. Just thinking."

"Good thoughts, I hope?"

Kat smiled. "Yes. Definitely."

"As I was saying, I'll need to return to Paris in a month to finalize everything with Belle Magazine. Would you like to join me?"

"Of course." Kat hesitated. "Do you mean as your assistant?"

"Yes, but this time it won't all be business. I'll make sure we get some time for some pleasure. I want you to finally see Paris properly. There are so many places I want to show you. And while we're over there, we can do whatever we want and go wherever we want without having to worry about anyone seeing us."

Kat's stomach fluttered. "I'd love that."

Lydia peered down at her, her eyes brimming with unexpected affection. "You know, in a few months' time, the deal with Belle Magazine will be finalized. It will win me some favor with the board, so I won't have to worry about my job so much. There'll still be the matter of your internship, but once it's over, we won't need to be so careful."

Kat's heart began to race. "I've been thinking about that too. About the future." She trailed off. What was it that she wanted to say?

Lydia looked at her curiously. "Yes?"

"I…"

Kat's heart beat even harder. She opened her mouth to speak, but all of a sudden, all her thoughts, her feelings, they seemed too complicated to put into words.

"I was just thinking it would be easier if we didn't have to sneak around," she said. "That's all."

Lydia smiled. "It would be, wouldn't it?" She raised her glass to her lips, finishing off her champagne. "Now, the room upstairs should be ready. Be a good pet and finish your drink."

Kat drank the last of her champagne down. "All done."

Lydia gave the leash a tug. "Let's go have some fun."

CHAPTER 18

Kat stepped into the room, following at Lydia's heels. They were above the club, in one of the many private rooms. Kat had been expecting some kind of medieval dungeon, but the room was surprisingly lush and elegant, with silk and velvet wall hangings and an array of plush fur and lace cushions and pillows, all the decor in deep, rich shades of purple and red.

But the luxuriousness of it all was in stark contrast to the items in the room. All around them were a variety of kinky toys and tools, along with some unusual furnishings that were clearly designed to restrain a person, including a large wooden cross and some kind of padded leather bench. All the equipment was covered with the same velvets, silks, and lace that the room was decorated with, but that did little to hide the fact that every item in the room was specifically designed for the singular purpose of erotic torture.

Kat's eyes fell to the bed at the center of the room, an enormous four-poster with silk sheets and sheer drapes hanging around it. Like everything else in the room, its lushness hid a more twisted side. At the bottom of the bed, underneath the mattress, was a cage.

Lydia spoke from beside her, making Kat jump. "Although that would be a fitting place for my kitten, I'm not going to put you in a cage. I chose this room because it's one of the few that actually has a bed." Her lips curled up into a smile. "You should see the other rooms. There are rooms where you can invite others to watch, or to join in. There are rooms designed to fulfill every naughty fantasy. My favorite is the medical room. It's full of all these delightful restraints and instruments."

Kat's pulse quickened. A few months ago, she would have been shocked by Lydia's suggestions. She still was, a little, but she was equal parts intrigued.

"But tonight, I want you to be comfortable," she said. "At least, as comfortable as one can be when tied to a bed."

Kat glanced at the bed again. This time, she noticed that the bed also had eyelets attached at various points on the frame, all a few inches apart. Presumably, these were for attaching ropes and restraints. She bit her bottom lip. Lydia was going to tie her up along with everything else?

Lydia's eyes flicked to the leather bag in the corner. "Good, my bag made it up here. I much prefer to use my own tools." She reached for Kat's wrists and unclipped the leash, along with the chain connecting the wrist cuffs together. "Bring it to me."

Kat obeyed.

Lydia set the bag down on the bed. "Now, as much as I like seeing you in that dress, you look better without it. Let me help you."

She took the hem of Kat's dress and pulled it up and

over her head in one swift motion, tossing it aside. Her eyes swept down Kat's body, hungry and approving.

She gestured toward Kat's bra and panties. "Those need to come off too."

As Kat stripped off her underwear, Lydia slid out of her skirt, leaving her in just the form-fitting corset, panties, and heels. Kat didn't even try not to stare. Lydia was hypnotizing. She still had her mask on, and underneath it, lightning sparked in her blue-gray eyes.

She reached for Kat's face and lifted the mask from her head, taking care not to tangle the string in Kat's hair. "There. Now I can really see you."

Lydia drew the back of her hand down Kat's cheek and kissed her delicately. Although Lydia's lips were gentle, Kat could feel the possessiveness in them, and in the unyielding press of Lydia's body against hers. When Lydia broke away, the storm in her eyes said the same thing. *You're mine.*

Lust surged within Kat's body. There was something about being desired so strongly, the way Lydia desired her, that sent a thrill through her.

"Are you ready, kitten?" Lydia asked.

All Kat could do was nod.

Lydia opened her leather bag and withdrew the short flogger she'd shown Kat that night at the hotel in Paris. She set it on the table next to the bed before pulling another item from her bag; a long, thin riding crop.

But she didn't stop there. She reached into the bag again, producing four red silk scarves, and laid them out on the bed.

"Onto the bed," Lydia said. "Lie down on your stomach."

Kat did as she was told. On her belly, naked, she couldn't

help but feel exposed. She propped up on her elbows, watching Lydia set a scarf at each corner of the bed.

"What's your safeword?" Lydia said.

Kat blinked. "Carnation." She'd forgotten all about her safeword. The reminder helped settle her nerves.

"Don't be afraid to use it. Remember, you're in control here. And while I'm going to take you right to the edge of your limits, I will never, ever break them."

Kat nodded, then added, "Yes, Mistress." There was something reassuring about addressing Lydia that way.

"Lie back down," Lydia commanded.

Kat lay on her stomach as one by one, Lydia bound Kat's wrists to the top corners of the bed, threading the silk scarves through the rings on the bedframe. She did the same for Kat's ankles, leaving her tied, spreadeagled, on the bed.

"Do those feel nice and snug?" Lydia asked.

Kat nodded. The bonds were tight, but not constricting. The silk felt smooth and cool against her skin.

"Close your eyes."

Kat shut her eyes, letting her cheek rest on the pillow beneath her. Lydia drew her hand down behind Kat's ear, tracing a line over the side of her neck and shoulder. "I'm going to take everything nice and slow," she said. "I want you to really enjoy this."

She pulled away. Kat held her breath. Was Lydia reaching for the flogger? The riding crop? Was she about to strike? What would it feel like? Would it feel good, like Lydia had told her?

But instead of the crack of a whip against her skin, she felt the whisper of Lydia's hand running down her back and over her bare ass cheeks. Lydia caressed them both firmly, before giving them a few testing slaps. Kat jolted with each one, her skin tingling all over.

After a few more spanks, Lydia pulled away again. Then, Kat felt the soft tails of the flogger between her shoulder blades. Lydia snaked it down Kat's back in a long, meandering line. Kat shivered, all the little tails on the flogger blending together like a brush, tickling her skin.

"Pain is a tool," Lydia said. "Just like everything in that bag of mine."

The flogger disappeared from Kat's back. She tensed.

Not a moment later, she felt the thud of the flogger's tails against her ass cheeks. She sucked her lip. The feeling wasn't what she expected. The pain was overshadowed by a tingly numbness.

She relaxed her body, sinking deeper into the bed beneath her, awaiting the next impact.

"Pain can be used to punish," Lydia continued. "It can be used to correct bad behavior."

Lydia snapped the flogger against Kat's ass again, harder this time. Kat sucked in a breath. This time, the pain was sharper, deeper, more intense. The heat of the blow seemed to spread over her whole body, setting it alight.

"It can be used to bring a submissive to her physical limits, pushing her body to a heightened state of awareness."

Lydia brought the flogger down again, even harder. Kat gasped. She was starting to reach the limit of what she could handle. But Lydia didn't push any further. She simply struck Kat again and again, in steady, rhythmic strokes, until every inch of Kat's body was overcome by a cool, burning sensation. A purr rose from her chest.

"And most importantly," Lydia said. "Pain can be used to enhance pleasure."

Lydia trailed the tails of the flogger between Kat's ass cheeks and down between her thighs. Kat trembled, a wave of pleasure emanating from deep below.

"This flogger is perfect for that," Lydia said. "It can be used to create many different sensations, not all of them painful."

Lydia ran the flogger up and down the insides of Kat's thighs, letting the tails brush the soft skin there. Kat let out a halting breath. She hadn't noticed her body's increased sensitivity. She was wet and throbbing already.

"Then there are other impact toys," Lydia said. "Toys that create a different sensation."

Her eyes still closed, Kat heard the thud of the heavy handle of the flogger on the table next to the bed, followed by silence. Then, Lydia's hand was at the back of Kat's shoulder, drawing her hair to the side, exposing the back of her neck.

Kat waited, the hairs standing up on her bare back. Something smooth and flexible pressed at the nape of her neck. *The riding crop.* Lydia traced it down the length of Kat's spine slowly, then flicked the crop against Kat's ass cheek, the sharp sting sending a shockwave through her. She shuddered from head to toe, overwhelmed with adrenaline and desire. Who knew that pain could feel so good?

Lydia snapped the riding crop against Kat's ass over and over. Kat bucked and writhed, sweet, hot pain running through her. Her mind blanked over as she drowned in all the sensations her Mistress lavished upon her.

Lydia massaged Kat's ass cheeks with her palms, letting her fingers slide into Kat's slit. A moan slid from Kat's lips.

"You see?" Lydia whispered. "Pain and pleasure, they complement each other. They're two sides of the same coin."

Kat murmured in agreement. She felt just as light and blissful now as she did when Lydia was pleasuring her. As Lydia continued to strike her with the riding crop, she fell so deep in a trance that when Lydia stopped, all Kat could do was whimper.

Lydia laughed softly. "I can see that you're enjoying this, but it's enough for now. I don't want to push you too hard. Right now, I know your limit better than you do."

She planted a kiss between Kat's shoulder blades, then unbound her legs and wrists.

"How was that, kitten?" Lydia slid into the bed next to her. "Feeling pleasure yet?"

Kat nodded. She felt incredible. The only problem was the deep, overwhelming craving she had for her Mistress that she was incapable of putting into words. She reached for Lydia blindly, clutching onto her as if her life depended on it. At that moment, it felt like it did. Kat *needed* her. She needed her Mistress to touch her and kiss her, to claim her as her own. And she wanted to do the same to Lydia.

"Lydia," she pleaded.

"What is it?" Lydia said. "Tell me what you want from your Mistress."

"I need…" Kat's mind was a fog of arousal. She ran her hand up Lydia's cheekbones, gliding her fingertips over the mask Lydia still wore. "I need you."

Lydia's expression softened. She removed her mask and

drew Kat in close, kissing her greedily, their arms twining and tangling. Lydia's thigh slipped between Kat's legs, stoking the burning fire within her.

Kat deepened the kiss, the hunger inside her taking over. Her hands wandered Lydia's body, exploring her curves and crevasses. She swept her fingertips over the lace of Lydia's corset, tracing lines over the corset's bones and the silky ribbons that laced it together. She skirted her hands down to where the corset met Lydia's panties, trying to pull them down. Lydia took Kat's hands and moved them away gently, eliciting a murmured protest.

Lydia pressed a finger to Kat's lips. "Patience, kitten."

Slowly, Lydia slid her panties down her hips and pulled them from her legs, before drawing Kat to her once again. Their lips collided, their bodies crashing together. Kat let out a pleasured sigh, melting into her Mistress. She felt the heat emanating from down in Lydia's center, tasted the longing in Lydia's lips.

She slipped her hand down to where Lydia's thighs met. She was slick and warm, even wetter than Kat. Kat slid her hand up and down Lydia's slit, letting her fingers glide over her tiny, hidden nub.

Lydia exhaled softly, parting her legs farther. "I need you inside me. Now."

Dizzy with desire, Kat slid her fingers down to Lydia's entrance, slipping them inside. Lydia tensed around her, then blew out a slow breath, her body relaxing. Kat eased her fingers in and out slowly, paying close attention to how Lydia's body reacted to her touch. After a few moments, Lydia began pushing back against her, grinding and rolling her body, her breath deepening. Kat let her guide the pace, thrusting in time with Lydia, her fingers growing more frantic as Lydia moved her hips faster.

"Oh, yes," Lydia whispered. "Faster."

As Kat picked up the pace, Lydia's hard pants turned to moans and her body began to shake. A second later, her walls tightened around Kat's fingers. Her head tipped back, and she cried out, undone by a bed-shaking climax that left Kat's hand and the bed beneath them wet with her arousal.

It didn't take long for her to recover. In the space of a few seconds, she was on Kat again, kissing her greedily. Her hand crept down between Kat's thighs, her fingertips grazing Kat's clit. Kat's feet and toes curled, digging into the bed beneath her. Her body was alight, every part of her primed for release. Making her Mistress come had only driven her closer to the edge.

As Lydia slid her fingers into Kat's entrance, her pleasure surged. It only took a few deep, deliberate strokes for Lydia to bring Kat to a climax. She arched against her Mistress, a cry flying from her lips as an unrelenting orgasm ripped through her. Her whole body shook, so lost in bliss that she was barely aware of her physical presence. She floated in a sea of ecstasy, with Lydia inside and all around her.

When her pleasure finally receded, she fell back down to her body and into Lydia's arms. Lydia caressed her face, kissing her with feather-light lips as awareness returned.

"How are you feeling?" Lydia asked.

"Incredible," Kat murmured. "Thank you, Mistress."

"You're welcome."

Kat wriggled out of Lydia's arms slightly, stretching out

her muscles. She let out a satisfied sigh. "I just want to lie here forever."

Lydia smiled, her blue eyes calm like the ocean. "I'm afraid I can't promise you that, but this room is ours for the rest of the night. We have plenty of time."

Kat snuggled in close to Lydia again, burying herself in her Mistress's body. As she closed her eyes, she felt a pang of longing. "Forever" wasn't possible for them, and not just in a practical sense. Everything between them was supposed to be nothing more than a fling.

But that line between a fling and something more became fuzzier with every kiss, every embrace, and Kat was starting to wish that line would just disappear altogether. Was she ready for that? Was she ready to give someone her heart again?

And, more importantly, did the enigmatic woman beside her want that too?

CHAPTER 19

Kat entered Lydia's office, shutting the door. Lydia looked up from her seat on the couch by the window, several documents spread out on the coffee table.

"Come here," she said. "I need to go over these slides you made for the presentation."

"Sure." Kat joined Lydia on the couch, taking care not to sit too close, just in case anyone happened to look into the office through the glass walls.

"I need you to make some changes to the opening. Let me show you."

Kat stared longingly at Lydia as she spoke. It felt like an eternity since that night at Lilith's Den. The Belle Magazine acquisition was well and truly in the works now, so Lydia was busier than ever. By extension, so was Kat. They didn't have a moment to spare at work. And outside of work, their interactions had mostly been limited to late-night phone calls.

But Kat craved so much more than talk. Her every waking moment, her every thought, was consumed by

Lydia. Whenever she walked into Lydia's office, she found herself wishing Lydia would follow through with her threat to tie Kat to her desk. Every time Lydia instructed her to do something, her head filled with the memory of Lydia commanding her to get on her knees, half-naked and bound.

Every time they were alone together, she remembered how good it had felt to have Lydia hold her aching body in her arms as she returned to herself in that bed at Lilith's Den.

She would give anything to experience that again. Not just the rush of submitting to her Mistress, but the feeling of having Lydia's arms around her.

"I need these changes finalized by tomorrow," Lydia said. "Can you do that?"

Kat blinked. "Right. Yes." She hadn't heard half of Lydia's instructions, but Lydia always wrote them down too.

Lydia cocked her head to the side. "Is everything all right?"

Kat nodded. "I was just distracted for a second."

Lydia gave her a sympathetic look. "I've been working you too hard, haven't I? You deserve a break." She looked at her watch. "Why don't you take lunch? I have that meeting across town soon, so I don't need you for anything right now. Take as long as you like. I won't be back for a couple of hours."

"Are you sure?" Lunch breaks were a luxury Kat could rarely afford.

"Yes. Consider it an order." Giving Kat a firm look, Lydia let her hand graze the top of Kat's thigh surreptitiously.

"You've served your Mistress well this week. Didn't I say I'd always reward you for that?"

Kat smiled, her cheeks growing warm. "Thank you, Mistress."

"I'll see you this afternoon."

Kat left Lydia's office, a spring in her step. As she headed back to her desk, she noticed someone standing by it, watching her.

Courtney.

Kat took a deep breath, willing the flush on her cheeks to disappear. She reached her desk and took a seat behind it. "Hi, Courtney. What's up?"

"Here." Courtney placed a stapler on Kat's desk. "I borrowed this earlier."

"Uh, thanks." Why had Courtney felt the need to return Kat's stapler at that exact moment? It was obvious that she wanted something. "Is there anything else?"

Courtney put her hands on her hips and stared down at Kat. "You and Lydia looked pretty close in there."

Kat's stomach flipped. She tried her hardest to keep her cool. "This again? I told you, I'm just doing my job. I'm Lydia's assistant. We have to work closely."

"Very closely, apparently."

Kat crossed her arms. "What are you implying?"

"I'm just saying, you two seem close. Almost intimately close."

"You're being ridiculous."

"Am I? Because you and her both, you know…" Courtney hesitated. "Like women."

"And what does that have to do with anything?"

"I didn't mean—" Courtney stumbled over her words

before gathering her composure again. "What I'm trying to say is, it kind of looks like something is going on between the two of you."

Kat raised an eyebrow. "You have to know how crazy that sounds."

"Does it, though? I mean, I get it. This internship is so competitive. Whatever it takes to get ahead, right?"

This time, Kat didn't have to fake her indignation. "Are you seriously accusing me of offering Lydia... *sexual favors* so she'll give me a job here after my internship?"

Courtney shrugged. "I don't know, maybe. Or maybe she seduced you. Or she coerced you." A look of concern crossed her face. "Is that it? Is she taking advantage of you?"

"Lydia wouldn't do that. She isn't some kind of predator. And there's *nothing* going on between us." Kat shook her head. She needed to end this. "Look, I don't know what you think you've seen, but you're imagining things. I'm not having this conversation with you. Just drop it."

Courtney spoke through gritted teeth. "Fine. But just know that I'm looking out for you, as well as all the other interns. If there *is* something going on between you and Lydia, it gives you an advantage. It's unfair to the rest of us. It's wrong, and you know it."

With that, Courtney turned and walked away.

Kat blew out a breath. She'd managed to throw Courtney off her trail, but only for now. As she grabbed her purse and left the Mistress offices to go down to lunch, she replayed all the conversations the two of them had had in her mind. It was clear that Courtney was getting more and more suspicious. Would she report Kat and Lydia? If she felt her chance of getting one of the coveted permanent roles here at Mistress was threatened, there was a real possibility that she'd expose them. But Courtney had no evidence.

Kat would have to keep it that way.

As she left the elevator and entered the lobby, she was so preoccupied with her thoughts that she almost didn't hear when someone called her name.

"Kat? Is that you?"

She froze in place. She knew that voice extremely well.

She turned slowly. Standing before her was a woman she'd spent months avoiding. And for the second time in weeks, their paths had crossed again.

"Brooke." Kat's jaw tightened. "What are you doing here?"

Brooke gave her a nervous smile. "Hi. I was working nearby. I heard you got a job at Mistress, so I thought I'd come and see you."

"You thought you'd stop by?" Kat's stomach churned with anger and irritation. "Are you seriously pretending this is just some casual encounter between friends?" She shook her head in disbelief. Why was she still standing there? Why didn't she just walk away, like she always did? She didn't owe Brooke anything.

Yet, something kept her there.

"Okay, fine," Brooke said. "You're right. There's nothing casual about this. I've been coming here on my lunch breaks in the hope that I'd get to see you. I really am working nearby. After I saw you at the party, I asked around and I heard you got the internship at Mistress. We've been so close all along and I didn't even know it. It was like a sign. I had to—"

"I don't want to hear it. I made it clear that I didn't want to see you or speak to you ever again."

"I know. But I needed to see you. I needed to speak to you. Ever since I ran into you the other night, I haven't been able to stop thinking about you." Brooke lowered her gaze, guilt written all over her face. "I never got the chance to tell you how sorry I am. For everything."

Kat crossed her arms. "Well, now you've told me. Goodbye."

"Wait," Brooke said. "Please, you have to hear me out."

"I don't have to do anything. I don't owe you anything. Not after what you did."

"I know! And I'm sorry. If I could take it back, I would. I miss you, Kat. I *need* you."

Kat scoffed. "Do you seriously expect me to get back with you?"

"I know I don't deserve you. I know I fucked up. But I promise I'll never do it again." Brooke looked hard into Kat's eyes. "Let me prove that to you. Just give me a chance."

As Kat stared back at Brooke, a realization came to her. All this time, she'd let her fury, her resentment toward Brooke build and build until she'd turned her into this monster in her mind, one who had shattered her life, her heart. Kat had blamed her for all the pain she'd been carrying with her all this time.

But as she looked back into Brooke's pleading eyes, she realized that Brooke wasn't the monster Kat had built her up to be. She was only human. And although Brooke had wronged her, she didn't hold any power over her. It was Kat herself that was causing all her turmoil by holding onto all her anger, letting it eat away at her until it threatened to consume her.

She needed to let go of it all.

"Enough." Kat steeled herself. She was ending this, once and for all. "For too long, I've dwelled on all the hurt you caused me. I let it poison me. But I'm finally moving on from all that. And if you ever loved me, you'll leave me alone so I can move on with my life in peace. I forgive you for what you did. I do. But that's all you're going to get from me."

Brooke's face fell. "You don't understand." She reached out and grabbed Kat's arm, her voice rising. "I can't let you go. Just give me another chance."

Kat tensed. Brooke's grip wasn't tight enough to hold her in place, but the wild, desperate look in her eyes made Kat freeze. Her heart thumped against her ribs. People were staring at them. She needed to get away.

"Kat. Is this woman bothering you?"

She felt a hand on her shoulder, firm and reassuring. *Lydia.*

Kat snapped out of her trance, yanking her arm out of Brooke's grasp. "No. We're done here."

Brooke glanced at Lydia. "Who's this?"

"That's none of your business."

"Wait." Brooke looked from Lydia to Kat and back again, her eyes widening. "Are the two of you together?"

"She's my boss," Kat said, a little too defensively.

Brooke's eyes widened. "I'm right, aren't I?"

Kat was a terrible liar, and Brooke knew her too well to be fooled. "It doesn't matter. It doesn't change anything."

"Then why won't you just listen to me? Please, just let me—"

This time, it was Lydia who spoke. "Kat has made herself clear. She wants you to leave her alone." Her voice dripped with venom. "I suggest you do so, or I'll be forced to call the building's security."

Brooke turned to Kat. "Please, don't do this."

Kat clenched her fists. She'd allowed Meghan to shield her from Brooke before, and now she was letting Lydia do the same.

She wasn't going to let anyone else fight her battles anymore.

"You've said what you wanted to say," Kat said. "And so have I. There's nothing more for us to talk about. You need to leave. And don't try to contact me again."

Brooke looked at Lydia one last time. Her shoulders slumped. "All right, fine. I won't bother you again. But just know this. I'm really sorry for what I did."

Kat remained silent and motionless until Brooke walked away.

Lydia turned to Kat. "Are you all right?"

"I'm fine," Kat replied. "Just a little flustered."

"Was that who I think it was?"

Kat nodded. "My ex. I just wasn't expecting to see her here. I don't know how she found me." And she was still flustered from her encounter with Courtney. Her whole body felt shaky.

"Kat." Lydia cupped Kat's cheek with her hand. "Just stop and breathe."

Kat took a few deep breaths, trying to calm herself down. She glanced around. People had stopped staring at them, and they were practically invisible in the crowded lobby, but they were still in public.

Lydia seemed to notice Kat's self-consciousness. She pulled her hand away. "Let's get out of here. Go somewhere quiet."

"But don't you have that meeting?"

"I'll reschedule it. It's not important."

Kat shook her head. "It's okay, really. You should go."

Lydia put her hands on her hips. "Last time I checked, I'm your boss, not the other way around. I'm canceling my meeting. We're going to take a long lunch together. This is non-negotiable."

Kat sighed. There was no arguing with Lydia. "Okay."

"Come on. I know the perfect place."

A short cab ride later, Kat and Lydia arrived at their destination, a sprawling Japanese garden hidden away in a quiet part of the city.

Kat looked around in awe as they walked through it. Ancient trees towered around them and neatly manicured bushes lined the path. They passed a pond filled with slowly swimming koi fish alongside an elaborate rock garden. Everything was tranquil and serene. It was almost like they weren't even in the city at all.

"This is beautiful," she said. "I didn't even know it was here."

"Not many people do," Lydia replied. "This place is private, with exorbitant membership fees, which keeps most of the city's residents out. But it's well worth the membership. It's my favorite place in the city." She steered Kat off the main path and onto a smaller one. "When I first moved here, I found I missed nature and wide-open spaces, so I came here often. Moving was a difficult transition for me. This became a sanctuary of sorts."

Kat peered at Lydia's face out of the corner of her eye as they walked. Whenever Lydia mentioned moving, her voice took on a tone that Kat couldn't quite decipher, something bittersweet and wistful. "Why was moving here so difficult for you?"

Lydia was silent for a moment. "It's a long story. Now isn't the time for it. Come on, I want to show you my favorite spot."

She led Kat over a red bridge that crossed a small stream. The only other people around were a handful of what seemed to be the garden's unobtrusive attendants. The only sounds were the whisper of the stream and the rustle of wind through the leaves of the trees, drowning out the noise of the city.

Finally, they reached a clearing, in the center of which was a small Japanese-style gazebo. They sat down inside.

"This is amazing," Kat said. "I can see why you like to come here."

"It's even lovelier at night. Perhaps I can show you sometime." Lydia put her hand on Kat's arm. "So, how are you feeling?"

"I'm fine, really. Just a bit rattled, that's all. I wasn't expecting to confront Brooke like that, today or ever."

"Do you want to talk about it?"

"I don't know. Honestly, I've avoided talking about her, or even thinking about her, for so long. I basically tried to erase her existence altogether. But it's obvious now that that was the wrong move. I've just kept everything I was feeling bottled up inside."

"What happened between you?" Lydia asked.

"Things got... messy. Brooke, she was my high school sweetheart. Everyone thought we were the perfect couple, that we were going to get married one day. But it all fell apart when I found her in our bed with one of our friends." Kat shook her head. "I thought that kind of thing only happened on TV. But no, it happened to me. Most of our friends knew she was cheating too. I have no idea if the time I caught her was the first time or the hundredth, but I didn't bother trying to figure it out. I just left. We haven't spoken since. Not until today. She came to the building looking for me."

Lydia's expression darkened. "Has she done this kind of thing before?"

"Well, when everything first blew up, she tried to get me to talk to her, but she gave up eventually. This is the first time in a while that she's tried to get in touch. I don't think I have to worry about her stalking me or anything. I know her, and she wouldn't do that. I think she just wanted closure. And to be honest, I needed closure too. But not from her. It was something I needed to find in myself."

Kat stretched her legs out in front of her, gazing absently at a lantern hanging from the roof as it swayed in the breeze. "At first, after everything happened, I blamed myself. I wondered if I'd done something wrong, if I wasn't enough for her. Eventually, I realized that it wasn't anything that I did. Brooke's actions were hers and hers alone. She's responsible for the choices she made.

"But after I realized that, I turned all my anger toward her. I channeled all my energy into hating her for what she did, and I let that anger eat me up." Kat's hands curled into fists. "But I don't want to live like that anymore. I don't want to be angry, and bitter, and sad. I don't want to be scared that anyone I get close to is going to betray me. I want to move on, but…" She shook her head. "I'm just not exactly sure how to do that."

Lydia took Kat's hand. "I'm sorry that all that happened to you. And I understand. Moving on from something like that isn't easy. It takes time for our wounds to heal."

"I guess you're right." Kat sighed. "You know, I think this has helped. Us, everything we've been doing together. Even before I ended things with Brooke, I felt like something was missing. It was like I was so lost in the relationship that I didn't have a sense of who I was. We'd been together for so long that I'd never gotten the chance to develop an identity of my own outside of it. I think that's why I had this idea that being single meant I could finally go wild and explore. What I really wanted was to find myself again."

Her gaze fell to her lap. "I feel like I've been able to do that with you. I've gotten to explore all these new parts of myself, to rediscover myself. Because of you, I've been able to figure out what I want, what makes me happy. I want to keep doing that, and I don't want my past to get in the way. I don't want it to hold me back anymore." She looked up at Lydia. "I want to follow this path and see where it leads."

Lydia squeezed Kat's hand. "I'm happy I've been able to help you rediscover yourself. And I'm here if you need me."

"Just having you with me is enough."

She glanced around. There was no one else nearby. She leaned toward Lydia and kissed her softly.

Lydia drew Kat into her arms, returning the kiss, her lips tender and slow. Butterflies flitted in Kat's stomach. Usually, when she and Lydia kissed, they were seconds from descending into a frenzy of passion. She'd had no idea that Lydia's lips could be so gentle and sweet.

After a moment, Lydia pulled away. "We have some time before we need to go back. Why don't we stay here and relax for a while? I'll have one of the attendants bring us some refreshments."

"Sure," Kat said. "I'd stay here all day if I could. I like it here. It's peaceful."

"You know what? Since I canceled that meeting, I don't have anything important on for the rest of the day. Why don't we take the whole afternoon off?"

Kat smiled. "I'd love that."

She leaned her head against Lydia's shoulder and closed her eyes. It felt good to get all that weight off her shoulders. And it felt good to open up to Lydia. And once again, she found herself longing for something more from her, more than this forbidden, secret fling.

She was getting ahead of herself. Letting go of her anger from her past relationship was one thing.

But learning to trust again, to open up her heart to someone? That was another.

CHAPTER 20

Kat stared vacantly out into the office. It was morning, and she was elbow deep in paperwork for Lydia. It was tedious, but it was still better than coffee runs, and it didn't require her to think. Naturally, she'd spent the last few hours daydreaming about Lydia.

She sighed. She'd been so certain that after everything with Brooke, she wouldn't be ready for another relationship for a long time. It was why she'd had little hesitation when it came to jumping headfirst into a fling with Lydia. She didn't expect to end up wanting anything more from her.

Yet, here she was, pining over Lydia, wishing for just a moment alone with her.

Kat rested her chin on her hands. She and Lydia had finally made plans to spend a night together over the weekend. She didn't know what it would involve. The two of them had talked about exploring some of Kat's other soft limits, but that was all. Lydia hadn't told Kat the specifics of what they were going to do, or where they were going to go. Kat had to admit, it added to her excitement.

Her laptop pinged, breaking her out of her reverie. It was an inter-office message from Lydia, asking Kat to bring her a file from her briefcase. Kat knew from her schedule that she was in a meeting with the other executives. She must have forgotten the file.

Kat sent off a quick reply and headed to Lydia's office. She opened the door and looked around until she spotted Lydia's briefcase by her desk, a chic red leather bag that looked vintage. Lydia had always had an amazing sense of style.

Kat opened the briefcase and searched through it until she found a thick file in the bag's inner pocket. That had to be it. As she took the file out, a small piece of paper fell out of the bag and onto the floor.

She picked it up. It was a note, handwritten in almost illegible looping cursive script. Her eyes were drawn to the bottom of the note. It was signed with a name, along with a small heart.

Kat frowned. The note obviously wasn't business-related. She had no reason to read it. But the personal nature of the note made her hesitate. She glanced around surreptitiously, then examined the note, carefully deciphering the handwriting.

My dearest Lydia,
Although we're apart, I'm still thinking of you.
I can't wait to have you back in my arms.
Emily

Kat's heart sank. Who was Emily? Why was she writing such intimate notes to Lydia? Was she a lover? Something more?

Her stomach lurched. Was Lydia involved with another

woman? After all, it wasn't like she and Kat had ever talked about having any kind of exclusive relationship. Weren't she and Lydia just having a fling? And hadn't Lydia herself said, in Paris, that she did what she did with Kat a lot, played those kinky games with women? Was she doing that with someone other than Kat?

Had there been someone else all along?

Kat's insides boiled, a storm building within her. The feeling was all too familiar. Was she being irrational, jumping to conclusions, because of everything Brooke had put her through? There was probably an explanation for it. There had to be.

But Kat couldn't imagine what it was.

Remembering herself, she slipped the note back into the briefcase and headed toward the conference rooms, trying to put the note out of her mind. But she just couldn't do it. That note, it wasn't the type that a friend or even a casual fling would write. It was intimate. Hadn't Kat already thought to herself she knew very little about Lydia's personal life? Although she'd never suspected Lydia of keeping secrets, now that she thought about it, there had been signs. Lydia had always been tight-lipped about her past. Was she hiding something?

Someone?

Kat shook her head. That was crazy. She was being crazy.

She reached the conference room. Lydia was inside, giving a presentation to the other Mistress executives. Kat entered the room quietly and handed her the file, ignoring the unease rolling around inside her. Lydia took the file, murmuring a thank you without even looking at her, and continued the presentation.

It was like Kat wasn't even there.

She left the room, seething inside. Was that all Kat was to Lydia, just an intern she could order to do her bidding, the same way she ordered her around in the bedroom? Did Kat mean anything to her at all?

She drew in a few deep breaths. She was overreacting. She was *not* going to let her emotions get the best of her. All she had to do was talk to Lydia, ask her about the note.

But what if she didn't like the answer Lydia gave her?

She returned to her desk, but she couldn't focus on work, too consumed by the doubt, the anger, the jealousy roiling inside. Why was this getting to her so much in the first place? She'd become far too invested in this fling of theirs. Had it been a mistake, letting her feelings get involved?

And fling or not, was Lydia just going to break her heart, just like Brooke had?

By the time Lydia finished her meeting, it was early afternoon. She'd barely made any headway on the work she had to do for the day, most of it related to the Belle Magazine acquisition and the plan to establish Mistress Paris. Somehow, she'd found herself helming both projects. She didn't mind. She enjoyed the challenge.

After refilling her coffee and stretching her legs, Lydia settled in behind her desk. She'd need to stay late tonight. She was so busy that for once, the idea of a late-night rendezvous with Kat in the supply closet didn't even cross her mind.

An hour or so later, Kat knocked on her office door. She let herself in and marched over to Lydia's desk, dropping a handful of letters on it. "Here's your mail. There are a couple of urgent letters on the top."

"Thank you," Lydia said. There were half a dozen other urgent tasks that needed her attention, so her mail would have to wait.

Kat lingered by Lydia's desk for a moment, before turning to leave. She was halfway to the door before Lydia realized something was amiss.

"Wait," Lydia said.

Kat sighed and turned back around.

Lydia leaned back in her chair and crossed her arms. "Why the rush?"

Kat shrugged. "I have work to do."

Lydia studied Kat's face. "Is something the matter?"

"Nope. Everything is great." Kat averted her gaze, refusing to meet Lydia's eyes. "Can I go?"

"No, you may not. Not until you tell me what's going on."

Kat scoffed. "Really? You're playing the boss card now?"

Lydia frowned. "What on earth has gotten into you?"

"Nothing." Kat pressed her lips together.

Lydia let out a hard sigh. "It's been a long day, kitten. I'm not in the mood for this. Just tell me what's going on."

Silence stretched out between them. Lydia stared back at Kat, waiting. It was entirely unlike her to behave this way.

Finally, Kat spoke.

"Who's Emily?"

Kat's words hit Lydia like a knock to her head. She grabbed hold of the armrests of her chair, a sudden dizziness overcoming her.

She swallowed the lump in her throat. "How do you know about Emily?"

"I found her note," Kat said.

Lydia's heart began to pound. "Where? Where is it?"

"In your briefcase. It fell out when I was getting that file for you."

Lydia looked at the bag beside her desk, the red briefcase she'd brought back from her old house. She grabbed the case and began searching through it frantically. "Where is it? What did you do with it?"

"Nothing," Kat stammered. "It's in the side pocket."

Lydia reached into the pocket, feeling around until her fingers grasped a small piece of paper. She pulled the note out of the bag. Sure enough, it was one of Emily's notes, one Lydia had found, read, and slipped back into her bag, long forgotten.

"I didn't know this was in here." She put the note down on the desk before her, staring at it blankly, struggling to hold back the torrent of emotions threatening to consume her.

"Lydia?" Kat's voice sounded distant. "Are you all right?"

Lydia looked up, snapping out of her trance. "I'm fine." She took the note and folded it up, slipping it into her pocket. "I don't want to talk about this now."

Kat frowned. "What's going on?"

"Just leave me," Lydia snapped. "I need space right now."

Kat flinched. "Okay. Fine."

As she headed for the door again, something clicked in Lydia's mind.

"Wait," she said. "Come back."

Kat paused for a moment, then turned back around. Her expression was hard and blank, but her eyes shimmered with hurt. Lydia felt a pang of guilt. She'd been so lost in her head that she hadn't realized what was so obviously going through Kat's mind.

"You're worried there's someone else," Lydia said.

"Well, is there?" Kat asked.

"It's... complicated." But now wasn't the time for excuses. She needed to tell Kat the truth. "We need to talk."

She got up from her desk and pressed the button by the door, dimming the glass walls of the office to opaque.

Lydia gestured toward the couch. "Sit. Please," she added.

Kat sat down tentatively.

Lydia took a seat beside her. "That note you found. It's from years ago. I didn't even know it was in the bag. I used to travel for work often, and Emily, she'd slip notes into my things for me to find whenever I was away." She paused. "Emily, she was my wife."

"So, you're divorced?" Kat asked. "Separated?"

"She passed away. It was a little over three years ago."

"Oh." Slow realization dawned on Kat's face. She covered her mouth with her hands. "I'm so sorry. I didn't know."

"It's fine. You had no way of knowing. I should have told you about her sooner. I've been planning to, but I just..." Lydia took a deep breath and let it out slowly. "The truth is, I've been avoiding telling you about her, telling anyone about her. I find it difficult to talk about her. But I should have told you sooner. I'm sorry."

Kat shook her head. "No, I understand. I didn't mean to force you to tell me about her."

"You didn't force me. You deserve to know about her, about the two of us. And it's time I told you everything."

Kat opened her mouth to speak, then shut it again, waiting for Lydia to continue.

"Emily and I, we met almost twenty years ago," she began. "We got together almost immediately, and we were practically married the entire time, although we couldn't legally get married until five years ago. We tied the knot officially as soon as we could. But then Emily… she…"

Kat put her hand on Lydia's, squeezing it gently. Lydia closed her eyes for a moment, gathering her thoughts.

"Emily got sick," Lydia continued. "It was cancer, the terminal kind. There were treatments, therapies, chemo, but all they did was delay the inevitable, drawing out her pain. It was difficult, seeing her like that. She was too young to be sick. And she'd always been so strong. It was hard seeing her so weak." Lydia's vision blurred, the beginning of tears filling her eyes. She held them back. "Eventually, Emily decided she'd rather live out the last of her days at home, with me. I was by her side until the end."

"I'm so sorry," Kat said. "I can't even imagine what that was like."

"It was difficult. After Emily's death, I was so lost without her. She was my everything, and she had been for most of my adult life. She was the only real family I'd ever had, and she didn't have any family either, so we were each other's entire worlds. And we weren't just a couple in the conventional sense. Our relationship, it was... she and I were..." Lydia's words caught in her chest. Was she ready to share something so intimate with Kat?

But Kat beat her to it. "Was she your submissive?"

Lydia nodded. "It wasn't just in the bedroom for us. It was in every element of our lives. Our existences were intertwined on so many levels that when she passed, I felt like I'd lost a part of myself." Her voice quivered. "It's been three years since then. It's taken me half that time to get to a point where the idea of a life without her became bearable, and it's taken me even longer to realize I need to start living again. That's why I moved here and took this job. I wanted to start a new chapter in my life." She gave Kat a small smile. "It hasn't been easy, moving on, but I'm getting there."

"Oh, Lydia," Kat said. "I'm sorry. About Emily, and about getting upset at you. You've been through so much. I just thought—" she shook her head. "I was wrong."

"No, I can see why you reacted the way you did. I know you've been hurt before." Lydia took Kat's hand in both of hers. "For the record, I would *never* do that to you. There's no one else. There's only you." She released Kat's hand. "Now, I need a moment alone. Can you give me that?"

Kat nodded. "Sure. And I'm sorry about Emily."

"Thank you."

As Kat left the room, Lydia took the note out of her pocket, reading it again. Despite her words to Kat, Lydia still hadn't shaken that nagging guilt, the feeling of betraying Emily. All those steps she'd taken toward moving on had taken her further and further from Emily.

She'd told Kat a lie, about herself and Emily. Just a small one, but a lie, nonetheless. She just hadn't been ready to make herself that vulnerable to Kat. Would she ever be able to do so? Would she ever be ready to move on when she was so clearly still stuck in the past?

And was it fair to Kat, the way Lydia was leading her on, when she didn't know the answer to it herself?

CHAPTER 21

Kat pulled her hair out of its ponytail. It was *not* cooperating. Giving up, she left it loose around her shoulders and looked at the clock on her nightstand. There were still a few minutes before she had to leave. She wanted her night with Lydia to be perfect.

She'd been worried, after everything that had happened, that Lydia wouldn't want to go ahead with their plans. Not only had Kat reacted badly at first, but Lydia had clearly been shaken by the situation. After Kat had left her office, Lydia had gone home from work early, disappearing completely. But the next day she'd returned to the office as her usual self, and everything between the two of them had gone back to normal.

Kat still felt awful about the way she'd handled everything. Her stupid trust issues had almost ruined everything. To think that Lydia had been carrying all this pain around, and Kat had brought it out, all because of her insecurities. She'd let jealousy consume her, and it had almost driven Lydia away.

Kat couldn't stomach the idea of losing her. While she'd been surprised to learn of Lydia's late wife, as soon as the truth about the situation had become clear, any jealousy she'd felt had disappeared. She could never be jealous of Emily. Lydia had been with her for almost two decades, then Emily had been taken from her prematurely. The scale of such a loss, it was beyond Kat's comprehension. She felt nothing but sympathy for Lydia.

And it explained a lot about Lydia. The way she'd always been so closed off, so cagey about her past. Despite Kat's lack of life experience, she understood that the death of a partner wasn't easy to move on from.

At the same time, it raised plenty of questions. Would Lydia ever be open to love again? She'd said she was ready to move on, to start fresh, but it was clear she still pined for Emily. It was only natural. Would her heart be forever closed? Would any other woman ever be enough for her?

Would *Kat* ever be enough for her?

There's no one else, Lydia had said. *There's only you.* Kat had no reason to doubt her words. She trusted that Lydia wouldn't betray her in the way Brooke had.

But what would it matter if the end result was the same —her heart shattered and her life in pieces once again?

Kat grabbed her purse and left her bedroom, finding Meghan in the living room, lounging on the couch while scrolling through her phone.

Meghan looked up at her. "Damn. Look at you, all dolled up."

Kat glanced down at her outfit. The skirt and top she wore hadn't come from a Paris boutique, but she thought she looked pretty hot. "I hope Lydia likes it."

"She will." Meghan set her phone down. "Why do you care all of a sudden? You're never this fussy about what you wear."

"No reason."

"Then why are you acting like a teenager going on a first date?"

Kat crossed her arms. "I am not. Okay, maybe I am. But it's only because tonight is going to be special."

"Special how?"

"I'm going to Lydia's place for the first time. It feels like a big deal."

That wasn't the only thing that made the night special. Lydia had already told her what the night would involve since it required some preparation. But Kat wasn't going to tell Meghan about that. As open as she was with her roommate, what she and Lydia had planned felt intensely intimate, and a little taboo, at least to Kat. That was part of the excitement.

"So, Lydia invited you to her place?" Meghan said. "Sounds like the two of you are getting serious."

Kat shrugged. "I don't know. Maybe."

"Would it be a bad thing if you were?"

"I don't know. It's just that everything is so complicated." Kat sighed. "You were right, you know. About everything with Brooke. It's been poisoning me. I thought I'd gotten over it, but then I almost screwed things up with Lydia because I was jealous, and now I'm not so sure if I'm ready for this."

"Oh, hun. The fact that you're even thinking about this is a good thing. It's progress. Maybe you aren't ready for another relationship yet. Maybe you are. But the only way you'll ever find out is if you let yourself feel whatever you need to feel. Don't let fear get in the way of exploring your feelings for Lydia."

Kat stared at her. "That's… really good advice." She hadn't expected something so thoughtful from a woman whose love life mostly involved picking up women at parties.

Meghan shrugged. "I'm a bartender. I spend a lot of time listening to drunk people's problems. We all have the same struggles. We're only human, after all."

"That much is true." Kat checked the time. "I should get going."

Meghan gave her a sly look. "So, should I assume you're not coming home tonight?"

Kat rolled her eyes. That was more like the Meghan she knew. "I don't know. And I didn't realize you needed to know my whereabouts at all times."

"Hey, I'm just looking out for you."

"Okay, Mom."

"Seriously, I am. I've been worried about you. I was starting to think that you were never going to be the same after everything that happened. But lately, I haven't felt like I need to worry about you so much. You seem happier. And I think that maybe it's because of Lydia." Meghan gave her a warm smile. "Have fun tonight."

Lydia checked the timer on the oven. It had half an hour left. It was the first time she cooked anything since moving in. Her lifestyle meant that she rarely had the time, nor did she ever need to.

So why had she chosen to cook for Kat tonight? She wanted to do something meaningful for her, something more personal than buying her expensive things to wear. And perhaps she simply felt the desire to share a small part of herself with Kat. When it came to the two of them, Lydia found more and more that she wanted to let down the hard mask she wore. Although it had become a part of her over time, it didn't change who she was underneath. Being with someone as sweet and gentle as Kat had helped her reconnect with her softer side, that part of herself that she'd buried deep all those years ago.

Lydia could no longer deny it. Kat wasn't just her intern. She wasn't just a way to escape, to find release. Kat meant so much more to her. Yet, she couldn't bring herself to tell Kat that, to say it out loud. That fear, that guilt about moving on from Emily was still there, and Kat finding Emily's note had brought it all to the surface.

Kat's initial reaction to finding the note had given Lydia pause. It was obvious that she had trust issues, and Lydia didn't blame her. Kat had been betrayed before. What she needed was someone whose love she wouldn't doubt, someone who could give her their whole heart.

But could Lydia ever give Kat what she needed when a piece of her heart was still with Emily?

Lydia's thoughts were interrupted by the intercom's chime. She headed to her front door and buzzed Kat up. While she waited, she straightened herself out in the hallway mirror. She wore a bespoke red lace dress and black heels, her hair flowing loose over her shoulders. Her corsets, her towering stilettos, were stowed neatly away in her closet. Tonight, she was a different kind of Mistress.

A minute later there was a knock on the door. Lydia opened it wide.

Kat stood in the doorway, looking irresistible as ever, a nervous smile on her face. She looked Lydia up and down. "Wow, you look... Wow."

"And here I was thinking the same thing about you," she said. "Come on in."

She ushered Kat inside, leading her to the living room.

"My apartment still needs some work. It's looking a bit sparse. I haven't gotten around to decorating yet."

Kat gaped around her. "Are you kidding? This place looks amazing. And it's huge."

It was true, Lydia's apartment was somewhat extravagant, but it was far smaller than the country mansion she was used to. However, now that she'd unpacked everything, it was starting to feel like home.

Kat wandered over to the wide living room windows, staring out at the city beneath them. "This view is incredible."

"It really is." Lydia joined her by the window, delighting in the awe that lit up the woman's eyes. "You should know, you're the first person I've invited over since I moved here."

"Really? I feel honored."

After giving Kat a few more minutes to take everything in, Lydia took her hand and drew her toward the couch, where a bottle of wine was waiting for them. She sat down and gestured for Kat to join her.

Kat peered down at her coyly. "I'm allowed to sit on the furniture now?"

"Only for tonight," Lydia said. "Your Mistress is feeling generous."

Kat took a seat next to her. Lydia poured two glasses of wine and handed one to her.

"Dinner is in the oven," she said. "It'll be another twenty minutes or so."

Kat stared at her. "You made dinner? Yourself?"

"What can I say? I'm a woman of many talents."

"I didn't know you could cook. You don't seem like the type." Kat waved her hand around the apartment. "I mean, look at all this."

"I wasn't born with a silver spoon in my mouth. I come from humble beginnings."

"Huh. That explains a few things."

"Like what?" Lydia asked.

"Like why you went nuclear on that sales assistant in Paris for being stuck up."

Lydia huffed. She'd forgotten all about that. "I simply can't stand that kind of snobbishness. There's nothing I hate more than people who look down on others."

As they waited for dinner, they fell deep into a conversation about nothing at all. It felt so thoroughly normal, so mundane, but Lydia couldn't think of anything she'd rather be doing. She was happy.

And didn't she deserve happiness? Didn't she deserve to start living again?

As the conversation lulled, they sipped their wine, a comfortable silence falling between them. Kat glanced in Lydia's direction, a curious look in her eyes.

"Can I ask you something?" Kat finally said.

"Go ahead," Lydia replied.

Kat hesitated. "Can you tell me about Emily? If you're comfortable talking about her, that is."

Lydia studied Kat's face. "Why do you want to know about her?"

"I'm just curious. You two were married, and before that, you were together for years. She's a big part of you. I want to know more about her, about the two of you."

Lydia took a slow sip of her wine. It had been a long time since Lydia had spoken of Emily with anyone. And Kat's curiosity seemed genuine.

"What would you like to know?" she said.

Kat thought for a moment. "How did the two of you meet?"

Lydia stretched herself out on the couch, gathering her thoughts. If Kat had been shocked about the fact that Lydia could cook, she'd be even more surprised to hear about Lydia's past. "We met at a department store. I was working there. She was a customer."

Kat's eyes widened. "You worked at a department store?"

"As I said, my life wasn't always like this. I grew up middle class, but my parents kicked me out when I turned eighteen. They'd always had a problem with my sexuality, so they cut ties with me as soon as they could. I was out on my own, working minimum wage jobs just so I could keep a roof over my head. I did that for years. And then, I met Emily."

The memory came to Lydia easily, although it was fuzzier than it used to be. "She came into the store to buy something. I don't remember what it was, but she asked me for advice, and we got talking. She came in regularly after that, just so she could see me, apparently. Finally, she asked me out one day. I turned her down the first time, but she didn't give up."

"Why did you turn her down?" Kat asked.

"I was intimidated by her. She was a few years older than me, and so beautiful and sophisticated. And as I later found out, she was incredibly wealthy. She seemed like she had it all. I was from a different world to her."

"I think I can relate to that," Kat murmured.

Lydia chuckled. "Well, after getting to know her a little, I realized we weren't so different. She had dreams, desires, fears, just like everyone else. And like me, all she really wanted was love and companionship. She had no living family, so we became each other's family. I moved in with her, and she gave me money to go to college so I'd be able to support myself if I wanted to. Emily was happy to support both of us. She had family money, enough so we'd never have to worry about our finances. But while she was content to live a life of leisure, I wanted more. So after I got my degree, I built a career for myself as a financial consultant, freelance, so we'd have the flexibility to travel. Some years we spent more time traveling than not. But we had to stop traveling when Emily got sick."

Kat gave her a small smile. "It sounds like you had an idyllic life together." She rested her hands under her chin. "What was she like?"

"She had a big personality, the kind of presence that took over any room she was in. Everyone adored her. And she was so strong, so fierce. That's why it was so hard for me after she was gone. She'd always been the strong one…"

Lydia's voice faltered. She was getting dangerously close to territory she wasn't sure she was ready to discuss.

"That's enough about Emily, for now," she said. "Tonight is all about you. I want you to enjoy yourself."

"I'm enjoying myself already," Kat said.

"Good, because I need you to be as relaxed as possible."

"Right." A flush rose up Kat's cheeks. She glanced down at her glass.

"Are you having second thoughts?" Lydia asked.

Kat shook her head. "Not at all. I'm just a little nervous."

"That's only natural. But I'll take care of you." Lydia placed her hand on Kat's arm. "You can trust me."

"I know, Mistress."

Kat leaned over to kiss her. As soon as their lips touched, the oven timer chimed.

Lydia drew back reluctantly. "We'll have plenty of time for that later." She rose from her seat. "First, dinner."

CHAPTER 22

An hour after dinner, Kat was naked in Lydia's bed, the outfit she'd so painstakingly picked out in a heap on the floor along with Lydia's dress. She stared at Lydia above her. Lydia still had her bra and panties on, a matching set made of delicate black lace. To Kat, she was just as alluring in lacy lingerie as she was in a corset and heels.

Lydia drew Kat up to her, kissing her with unusual softness. She trailed her hands down Kat's body, sweeping them over her curves, her fingers tickling and teasing Kat's skin. A sigh whispered through Kat's body. Lydia's touch was heavenly.

She slipped a finger between Kat's thighs and traced it up her stomach, leaving a trail of wetness behind. "All warmed up now?"

"Yes, Mistress." Lydia hadn't skimped on the foreplay. Kat was as ready as she'd ever be, but her heart still fluttered with the thought of what was to come.

Lydia cupped Kat's chin in her hand. "Just relax. Let your

Mistress take care of everything. Tonight is all about making you feel good."

Kat nodded. Lydia got up from the bed and stripped off her bra and panties, then walked over to a nearby chest of drawers. She opened the bottom drawer and produced a leather strap-on harness, along with a small dildo. She slipped the dildo into the O-ring at the front of the harness, then slid it up her legs.

Once the harness was secured around her waist, Lydia returned to the bed, gazing at Kat with lust-filled eyes. "Are you ready, kitten?"

"Yes, Mistress," Kat murmured.

"On your hands and knees."

Kat did as she was told, her heart racing. Lydia joined her on the bed, kneeling beside her. She drew her finger down the length of Kat's spine, all the way from her neck to her tailbone, sending a shiver through her.

"You look so enticing like this." Lydia let her hand graze Kat's ass cheek. "Perhaps I should have you follow me around on all fours from now on."

Kat exhaled slowly and closed her eyes. As usual, Lydia's erotic threats only inflamed her, but they didn't help settle her nerves.

Getting into position behind her, Lydia slipped a finger up to the peak of Kat's thighs, rolling it over her clit. A jolt of pleasure went through her. At the same time, she felt a thick droplet of cold liquid trickle down her tailbone and between her cheeks. She shivered.

Lydia slid her finger up Kat's slit, all the way back to her rear entrance, mixing her wetness with the slowly warming lube.

"I'm going to take it nice and slow," she said softly. "Just relax. And don't forget to breathe."

Kat nodded. Lydia shifted behind her, the hard strap-on brushing against the inside of Kat's thigh. Kat stiffened before remembering Lydia's words. *Relax. Breathe.* She took a deep breath, then another, but despite her arousal, she still felt tense. Her fingers curled in the sheets beneath her, her pulse speeding up. Was it time for her to use her safeword? She never expected she'd need to use it, let alone for something so mundane.

But before she had the chance to speak, Lydia touched Kat's shoulder gently. "What's the matter, kitten?"

Kat sucked on her bottom lip, trying to sort out her thoughts. "I'm not sure…"

"Turn around. Look at me."

Kat turned and sat, tucking her legs underneath her. She looked up at Lydia. Lydia had a stern expression on her face, but her eyes were full of concern.

"You're too tense. You need to be relaxed for this."

"I know," Kat said. "I guess I'm a little nervous."

"We don't have to do this. Do you want to stop?"

Kat shook her head.

"Then tell me what you need. Tell me what you want from your Mistress."

"I don't know." She wanted this, but she didn't understand why she was finding it difficult.

"Yes, you do." Lydia took Kat's hand. "Close your eyes. Listen to your body. What does it feel? What does it want?"

Kat shut her eyes, trying to sift through all the emotions simmering inside her. Anxiety. Uncertainty. Anticipation.

But underneath it all, somewhere deep within, was an overwhelming need for Lydia.

"I want..." She opened her eyes, looking back at her Mistress. "I want to feel you with me. I want to be close to you."

Lydia squeezed Kat's hand. "Now that wasn't so hard, was it? I have just the thing for that."

She reached for the nightstand and opened up a drawer, producing a long silk scarf. Kat frowned. It was just like the scarves Lydia had used to tie Kat up that night at Lilith's Den. Being bound was the opposite of what she wanted right now.

Her reluctance must have shown.

"I'm not going to tie you up," Lydia said. "Do you remember what we talked about that night in Paris? About how restraints take away a submissive's power, giving her the freedom to surrender?"

Kat nodded.

"I've noticed that's especially true of you. Whenever I have you all bound up, you're far more relaxed. But tying a submissive up isn't the only way to take away her power." Lydia held the satin scarf up before her, stretching it between her hands. "Close your eyes. Trust me."

Kat closed her eyes. Tonight was all about exploring limits, and while this was pushing hers, she could handle it. As long as she could still move. As long as she could still feel her Mistress.

Lydia pushed Kat's hair over her shoulders, gathering it at the back of her neck. Carefully, she wrapped the blindfold around Kat's eyes, tying it in a knot at the back of her head. Kat's breaths slowed and her ears pricked, her mind trying to compensate for the sudden darkness.

"Do you see now?" Lydia said. "Without your sight, you are at the mercy of your Mistress. You have no choice but to rely on me, to focus on me alone. You are forced to let go of all your thoughts, all distractions, all your fears and worries." She pushed Kat's shoulders down to the bed and leaned over her, letting her lips graze Kat's ear. "All that's left is me, your Mistress, and you, that part of you that longs to yield to me."

Lydia kissed her again, her lips demanding and possessive. Kat crumbled underneath her, all anxiety dissipating. Slowly, Lydia became her whole world, overpowering all her senses. She immersed herself in Lydia's touch, her voice, her taste. Her tongue and lips were sweet and sharp as wine, and just as intoxicating.

Lydia whispered a command into Kat's ear, prompting her to roll onto her side, facing away from her. She cradled Kat's body in hers from behind, her lips velvet-smooth against the back of Kat's neck, her skin warm against Kat's skin. Kat curled against her. She could feel Lydia's heartbeat, the rise and fall of her chest with each breath, the press of the strap-on against the small of her back. She inhaled deeply, letting Lydia's scent envelop her.

Her hand wandered forward, over the swell of Kat's breasts. Her fingertips skimmed Kat's nipple, working it into a hard peak. A soft moan fell from Kat's mouth.

"That's it," Lydia said. "Listen to your body. Feel what it feels. Your body craves me."

She slid her hand down, over the curve of Kat's hipbone,

all the way to where her thighs met. She was wet and aching, the slight brush of Lydia's fingertips sending tremors through her. She resisted the urge to arch into Lydia's hand. She needed to feel her Mistress's body against hers.

"You long for your Mistress." Lydia's voice echoed in Kat's ear. "You long to yield to me."

Kat shuddered against her, desire taking over. She was ready.

Her fingers still working Kat's clit, Lydia shifted her hips, drawing the strap-on up to the apex of Kat's thighs. She slid its tip between Kat's lower lips before bringing it up to probe gently at her rear entrance. Kat reached back blindly to grab hold of Lydia's hip, anchoring herself to her.

Yield to me, Lydia said silently. All of a sudden, it felt like an easy thing to do. She'd already given Lydia so much of herself, so many parts of her that she'd never shared with anyone else. This was no different.

She drew in a long, slow breath, anticipation growing within her, the ache between her legs growing with it. When Lydia finally entered her, it was with painstaking slowness, easing her way in carefully. Kat gripped harder at Lydia's hip, prompting her to pause.

Kat took a few more deep breaths, relaxing into the new sensation, then loosened her grip on Lydia's hip once more. After giving her a moment to adjust, Lydia took hold of Kat's waist and slid deeper into her, until she was buried to the hilt. Kat quivered, all her tension giving way to pure, concentrated pleasure. The fullness inside her was unlike anything she'd ever experienced.

"How does that feel?" Lydia said, her voice caressing Kat's ear.

"Good." Kat's words came out strangled and strained. "So... good."

Lydia pulled Kat tighter into her, locking Kat's body against hers. The movement caused the strap-on to shift deep within Kat, sending pleasure lancing through her. Lydia slid her hand between Kat's thighs again, strumming Kat's clit as she moved inside. Kat trembled feverishly, her eyes tipping back into her head. The dual stimulation seemed to amplify all the sweet sensations she was feeling.

Lydia rolled her hips faster, thrusting harder, sending jolts of electricity into Kat's core. She let out a whimpering moan, her hand scrabbling at Lydia's hip, her fingers digging into Lydia's flesh. But this time she was urging Lydia on, not trying to slow her down. She felt ready to burst, but her pleasure kept intensifying, climbing to new heights, penetrating hidden, untouched parts of her.

When she finally reached a climax, it arose from deeper within her than ever before. A shudder rippled through her, every nerve in her body afire. Lydia held her tightly, still inside her, her fingers working Kat's clit, holding her in a state of orgasmic bliss for what felt like an eternity.

Only when Kat had had every last drop of pleasure drained from her, Lydia eased away and took Kat's face in her hands, stroking her cheek with her thumb. "You did so well, kitten."

As she drew Kat into a tender, aching kiss, Kat came apart, losing herself in her Mistress's welcoming body. She never wanted to leave this bed. She never wanted to leave Lydia's arms.

She felt a stirring in her chest. This wasn't the first time she'd felt this way, like she wanted to spend an eternity like this, with Lydia.

But it wasn't until that moment that she realized what that feeling was.

CHAPTER 23

Kat lay across the couch, her head in Lydia's lap, Lydia stroking Kat's head idly. They'd spent most of the morning in bed, as well as much of the afternoon. Kat let out a sigh. This contentment she felt, the warmth in her chest, the yearning to be near Lydia—it all pointed to one thing.

How had this happened? *When* had this happened? When had her feelings for Lydia grown into something too strong for her to ignore?

When had her heart begun to ache for Lydia just as much as her mind and body?

She peered up at Lydia. Lydia was still stroking Kat's hair, but she had a vacant look in her eyes.

"Lydia?" she said.

Lydia blinked. "Yes, kitten?"

"Is everything okay?"

Lydia nodded. "I was just thinking."

"Good thoughts, I hope?"

Lydia's response was to draw Kat up, kissing her gently.

Kat dissolved into her. She was still feeling open and vulnerable from the night before, but in a good way. Together, with Lydia, Kat had broken past all her limits, and it was utterly freeing.

She deepened the kiss, letting her hands stray up the front of Lydia's body, all the way to the collar of her robe. She drew it open slightly, struck with the sudden urge to feel Lydia's skin against hers, to explore and pleasure her, to have Lydia do the same.

Lydia pushed Kat away half-heartedly. "Don't tell me last night and twice this morning wasn't enough for you."

"What can I say?" Kat murmured. "You really make me want you."

Lydia shook her head, a hint of a smile forming on her lips. "I'm going to have to do something about your insatiable appetites. Perhaps I'll tie you up and make you come so many times that you'll beg me to stop." She glanced toward the dining room. "I've been wondering what you would look like bound to my dining table."

Kat's face grew hot. Surely this was another of Lydia's perverse threats intended to make Kat blush.

But the look in Lydia's eyes said otherwise. "Go to my bedroom. In the bottom right drawer of my chest of drawers, you'll find some rope. Bring it to me. Four lengths should be enough."

Murmuring a "Yes, Mistress," Kat got up from the couch and wandered back to Lydia's bedroom. As she stepped through the doorway, she looked around her. When she'd been in the bedroom with Lydia earlier, she'd been preoccupied, so she hadn't had the chance to examine the room closely. There was a large walk-in closet to the side, bursting with stylish designer clothes, and the adjoining bathroom was full of luxury products. In the bedroom itself, the bed, still in disarray from the night before, was similar to the four-poster bondage bed in the room in Lilith's Den, only the design was more subtle, the tie points less obvious.

Kat remembered herself. She needed to hurry up. Her Mistress was waiting, after all. As she located the chest of drawers, she noticed an ornate wooden dressing table next to it. She ran her fingers over the elaborately carved wood, surveying the array of Lydia's things on top of the table.

There was a pair of garnet earrings that Kat had seen Lydia wear to work. A hairbrush with several strands of fine auburn hair curled in its bristles. A delicate glass perfume bottle, only a third full.

Kat picked up the bottle of perfume and held it to her nose, closing her eyes and breathing in deeply. It was like the essence of Lydia, that intoxicating scent that had Kat weak at the knees every time Lydia passed her by in the office.

She put the bottle down. Beside it was a large silver jewelry box. Kat opened it up, peering inside. The box didn't contain just jewelry. It held a collection of photographs and trinkets.

Kat picked up the topmost photograph. It was a picture of two smiling women on their wedding day. One of the women was Lydia. The other had to be Emily.

So this was Emily. She was beautiful, and she looked happy, full of life. Lydia looked happy too. Kat had only seen her smile like that a few times. This morning, when they'd woken up next to each other, was one of them.

Her eyes fell to the rest of the contents of the box.

Among the trinkets was a thick leather collar. Kat knew what that collar meant. It must have belonged to Emily. Were all the items in the box keepsakes related to Emily? Kat had to admit she was curious about her. So much of what Lydia had told her about Emily had been unexpected. Kat wanted to know more.

However, it was obvious that the box and its contents were private. Looking through it without Lydia's permission felt wrong.

As she reached out to shut the lid of the box, she noticed something, a photograph underneath the collar. She took the collar out of the box, followed by the photograph, and held both up before her. The photo was a Polaroid of Lydia and Emily, the two of them sitting side by side, Lydia's head resting on Emily's shoulder.

Kat looked at the collar again. The very same collar was in the photo.

But it wasn't Emily who was wearing it.

Lydia's words echoed in her mind. *Emily had always been the strong one.*

Emily hadn't been Lydia's submissive.

Lydia had been hers.

Kat stared at the photo. It all made sense. Lydia had always spoken of submission with such intimacy, like her knowledge of it was personal. It was because she had experienced that surrender herself. She knew what it was like to be where Kat was, to feel all the things Kat felt. She had been Emily's submissive. Emily had been her Mistress.

But why had Lydia lied to Kat about it?

"Kat? Are you in there?"

Kat turned toward the door, just in time to see Lydia

enter the room. Kat dropped the photo and the collar back into the box.

But it was too late.

Lydia froze inside the doorway, her face contorting into a mask of pain.

"Lydia," Kat said. "I—"

Lydia's expression grew dark. She marched up to Kat, shut the lid of the silver box, and snatched it up. "What do you think you're doing?"

Kat took a step back. "I'm sorry! This isn't what it looks like. I just—"

"You just what? You went looking through my things?" A scowl formed on Lydia's face. "Again?"

Kat's stomach sank. "It isn't like that."

Lydia hugged the box to her chest. "Was it even an accident, you finding that note in my bag? Have you been doing this all along? Digging through my private things?"

Kat shook her head. "I would never do that. I'm sorry, I was just curious about Emily and—"

"Are you jealous of her?"

Kat flinched like she'd been struck. "No, of course I'm not."

But it was like Lydia didn't even hear her. "I should have known. You said yourself that you have trust issues. Is this why you were asking me about Emily last night? Because you're jealous?" She narrowed her eyes, her gaze boring into Kat's skull. "Or are you trying to replace her?"

Kat felt a sharp stabbing in her gut. "No." How could Lydia say these things? "I would never, ever try to replace her. Lydia, please!" She looked back into Lydia's eyes. They were so hard and cold.

It was like she was looking at a stranger.

Kat swallowed. "I'm sorry," she whispered. "I just... I'm sorry."

Before Lydia could speak again, Kat turned and ran out of the room. She grabbed her things. She needed to get out of there. As she opened the front door, she heard Lydia calling her name. She stopped in the doorway, just for a moment, but she couldn't ignore the sinking in her chest and the tears welling in her eyes.

She left Lydia's apartment, shutting the door behind her.

CHAPTER 24

Kat typed away furiously on the keyboard, working through Lydia's emails like she did every morning. It was Monday, and she was back at work. Lydia, on the other hand?

She was nowhere to be found.

Kat scowled at her laptop screen, fuming. She hadn't heard from Lydia at all since the fight they'd had at her apartment, and to top it off, she hadn't come into work. Kat had access to Lydia's schedule. Lydia was supposed to be in the office today. She simply hadn't shown up. Kat didn't know why, and she didn't care.

She sighed. That wasn't true at all. Kat *did* care. That was the problem. She cared so much about Lydia. But then Lydia had said all those horrible things to her, before ghosting her completely.

Something clenched in her chest. She was hurt. She was angry. But more than that, she felt the sting of rejection. She'd taken this leap of faith with Lydia, trusting Lydia to lead her on a journey to explore all her deepest desires,

desires that she'd hidden even from herself. She'd made herself vulnerable to Lydia, time and time again, in ways more intimate than anything she'd ever done before.

And that night in Lydia's bed, she'd finally overcome all her fears and admitted to herself that she had feelings for Lydia.

Then Lydia had accused her of trying to replace Emily.

Where had such an accusation come from? Sure, Kat had snooped around, looked through things she shouldn't have. And it was true, she had insecurities about her and Lydia. Was Lydia right? Was Kat jealous of Emily? Had everything with Brooke twisted her so badly that she'd turned into this miserable, resentful person, incapable of trust?

Kat shook her head. Lydia was wrong. She wasn't jealous of Emily, and she certainly wasn't trying to replace her. Lydia had overreacted. Kat was right to feel the way that she did.

But why had Lydia reacted so strongly in the first place? When Lydia had held the jewelry box in her hands, behind all the anger in her eyes, there had been this deep, unmistakable pain. Did it have to do with the secret Kat had discovered, the fact that Lydia had been Emily's submissive? Sure, it was unexpected, but it didn't warrant Lydia's reaction.

Was there an explanation for everything? Maybe if Kat just reached out to her, talked to her, she could find out what was going on. But the thought of facing Lydia, after the way Lydia had looked at her, was too painful.

Could they ever come back from this, or was everything between them broken beyond repair?

"Katherine?"

Kat looked up from her desk. Angela, the internship supervisor, stood before her, a folder in her hands and a grave expression on her face.

"I need to speak with you," she said. "Come with me."

Her mind still on Lydia, Kat got up and followed Angela into one of the nearby conference rooms. It was empty.

Angela sat down at the conference room table and gestured to the chair across from her. "Take a seat."

Kat pulled out the chair and sat down tentatively. What was going on?

Angela cleared her throat. "Look, you've been an excellent intern, so I'm not going to beat around the bush." She folded her hands on the table before her. "It's been brought to the attention of management that you and Lydia Davenport are engaged in some kind of… intimate relationship."

Kat's heart plummeted from her chest. *No.* This wasn't happening. It couldn't be happening. Why? Why now?

"Another employee reported their suspicions," Angela continued. "Most of the evidence they presented was dubious at best, but they provided a photo of the two of you together."

A lump formed in Kat's throat. "A photo?"

Angela hesitated. "It's nothing compromising. But it shows the two of you interacting in a manner that can only be described as unprofessional." She opened the folder she was holding, pulling out a photograph. "Here."

She slid the photo across the table. It showed Kat and Lydia in the lobby of the Mistress building, Lydia's hand on Kat's cheek. The two of them were standing so close that their bodies were almost touching. Kat's stomach iced over. It must have been taken the day that Brooke had shown up.

The photo had captured the brief moment when Lydia had comforted her after Brooke had left. How had someone who worked at Mistress managed to walk by at that very moment, catching it just by chance?

Unless it hadn't been chance. Unless the photo had been taken by someone who was already suspicious of them, someone nosy enough to follow them in order to find evidence of their secret affair.

Someone like Courtney.

"Before we move on, do you have anything to say about these allegations?" Angela asked. "Are they true?"

Kat looked down into her lap. Lying to Courtney, dodging her insinuations, was one thing. But lying to her supervisor, denying her relationship with Lydia in the face of clear evidence?

She couldn't bring herself to do it.

"Yes," she said quietly. "It's all true."

"That is... unfortunate," Angela said. "The situation is currently under investigation by management, but given that you've confirmed these allegations, it's inappropriate for you to continue with your internship. I'm sorry, but the possibility that your relationship with a superior could give you an unfair advantage is too high. Personally, I don't believe that you or Lydia would allow that to happen. But the internship program here at Mistress is highly coveted and well respected in the industry. The board feels that the optics of this situation alone are a problem for the company."

Angela continued, but Kat barely heard a word she said. Her dream job had been within her reach, only for it to be snatched away in a matter of seconds. A numbness came over her. Her whole world was crumbling to pieces.

"As of today, your position in the internship program has been terminated," Angela said. "You'll receive severance pay, as per your contract. Now, I'll need your staff access card."

Kat blinked. Angela was holding out her hand, waiting. Mechanically, Kat unclipped her ID card from her waistband and handed it over.

"I'll take you to your desk so you can clean it out," Angela said.

Kat followed Angela out of the conference room and back to her desk, her head in a daze. As she packed her things under Angela's watching eye, she glanced toward Lydia's office. It was still empty. Was that why Lydia wasn't here? Had she been fired too?

"Lydia," she said quietly.

Angela frowned. "I'm sorry?"

"Lydia. What happened to her? Did she get fired?"

Angela hesitated.

"Please, I have to know."

Angela sighed. "Look, I don't know the details. Most of this investigation is above my head. But as far as I know, Lydia still has a position here."

"Oh."

At least Lydia's job was safe. After all, Lydia had been so worried about the board getting rid of her if they found out about her and Kat. But did she know that Kat had been fired? She had to know. And if she did, why hadn't she warned Kat? Why hadn't she said something to her?

Why wasn't she here?

Seemingly noticing Kat's distress, Angela gave her a sympathetic look. "I'm sorry. That's always how these things turn out. It's whoever is lowest down on the ladder that suffers the consequences." Her expression returned to its serious state. "Now, are you finished? I need to escort you from the building. It's company policy, nothing personal."

Kat nodded dumbly. As she walked through the office for the final time, she felt dozens of eyes on her. When she passed the interns' desks, the stares were accompanied by whispers. All the interns were watching her, except for one —Courtney. She was avoiding Kat's gaze completely. Was that guilt on her face, or triumph? Kat didn't know, and she didn't care.

Angela led Kat to the elevator, and they rode it down to the ground floor. It was only when they were standing before the lobby doors that Angela bade her farewell and retreated, letting Kat continue alone.

She looked back over her shoulder, then left the building for the last time. It was all over. Her dreams of working at Mistress had been crushed. As she struggled to keep herself together, she desperately wished to be in the arms of the one person whose presence had always made her feel secure and comforted.

But Lydia had disappeared.

Kat was all alone.

CHAPTER 25

Lydia sat slouched on the couch in her living room, the silver jewelry box on the coffee table before her. She hadn't touched it since the moment she'd taken it from Kat, sending her sprinting out of the apartment.

Since that afternoon, Lydia had spent her days wandering her apartment listlessly. She'd taken off work, and she'd shut out the world, unable to face it. She was paralyzed by the weight of her guilt.

And she couldn't bear to face Kat.

She felt a tugging deep in her chest. The moment she'd seen Kat holding the collar, that precious symbol of what Lydia and Emily had shared, something inside her had unraveled. Her mask had been stripped away, and she'd been forced to confront the fact that she was leaving Emily and everything that collar represented behind. She'd started a new life. She'd changed into a completely different person. She'd begun to find happiness. She'd started to forget Emily.

But most of all, she'd fallen for Kat. Wasn't that the ultimate betrayal of Emily's memory?

Lydia couldn't handle the guilt. She'd let it all spill out of her, and she'd directed it at Kat. Everything she'd accused Kat of had been what she'd feared that she, herself, was doing. It was Lydia who was betraying Emily, Lydia who feared she was replacing Emily with Kat. Kat had been entirely innocent.

She'd give anything to take back what she'd said and done. She wanted so badly to fix things between them.

But after the way she'd handled everything, lashing out at Kat, falling apart, one thing was clear—she wasn't ready to move on. It had been selfish of her to string Kat along when she'd always known this was true.

Lydia closed her eyes. After all this time, she was still faking it. She wasn't strong. She wasn't in control. She was the same lost girl she'd been when Emily had found her, the same helpless woman she'd been when Emily had left her. She didn't know how to do this alone.

The buzz of the intercom pulled her out of her stupor. She tried to block it out, but the buzzing didn't stop. Sighing, she got up from the couch and dragged herself to her front door. The intercom screen showed Yvonne standing downstairs, her arms crossed, an impatient expression on her face.

She buzzed Yvonne up. Had Lydia missed something important at work? Her phone had to have died by now too. She'd lost track of time entirely. It was evening now. Had she missed two full days of work?

She felt a twinge of guilt. She'd always had a habit of coping with her problems by shutting the world out. It hadn't caused any issues in the past, when she'd lived a more solitary life, but now she had a job, responsibilities, people who relied on her. She couldn't do things like this anymore. The CFO of a multi-billion-dollar company couldn't just disappear for days on end without warning.

A minute later, Yvonne knocked on Lydia's front door. As soon as Lydia opened it, Yvonne practically pushed her way inside.

"Lydia, thank god," Yvonne said. "We've been trying to get a hold of you since yesterday."

"I'm sorry," Lydia said. "My phone died. Did I miss something important?"

Yvonne's brows drew together. "You don't know, do you?"

Lydia frowned. "What's happened?"

"We should sit down."

Lydia led Yvonne to the living room. They took a seat on the couch. A feeling of dread came over her. Something was very wrong.

"It's about your intern," Yvonne said. "Kat. One of her coworkers reported that the two of you are in an intimate relationship."

Lydia cursed under her breath. It had finally happened. They'd been caught.

"The board caught wind of the situation, and things have gotten messy," Yvonne continued. "Rest assured, your position is safe. Given your work with the Belle acquisition, the board is convinced that you're far too valuable to the company to be let go over something like this. But Kat's job is a different story." She paused. "Kat was questioned. She admitted that the allegations are true. As a result, she was let go from the internship program."

Lydia's stomach lurched. Kat had been fired? "When did this happen?"

"Yesterday morning."

Lydia cursed again. Kat must have been devastated. And where had Lydia been this entire time? Here, moping in her apartment. She'd been so lost in her head, mired in self-pity, that she'd abandoned Kat when she needed her.

Her heart sank. Had Kat tried to reach out to her, only to find herself ignored? Or worse—had she been so upset by what Lydia had said to her on the weekend that she hadn't even bothered? Did she think that Lydia simply didn't care that this had happened?

Lydia collapsed onto the couch and clutched her head in her hands. How had everything between them fallen apart so quickly?

"Are you all right?" Yvonne asked.

"I need to fix this," Lydia said. "I need to make everything right."

"You're not just talking about her job, are you?"

Lydia shook her head.

Yvonne studied her. "You really care about her, don't you? When I heard there was something between the two of you, I wasn't sure if it was serious or not."

"It wasn't, not at first. But everything has changed, and I drove her away…"

"What happened?" Yvonne asked.

"I said things to her. Awful things that I can't take back. And even if I could, it wouldn't fix the real problem."

"What do you mean?"

"I'm not ready for this," Lydia said. "I'm not ready to

move on. I want to, but whenever I try, I just can't help but feel like I'm betraying Emily."

"Emily? She was your wife?"

Lydia nodded.

"I see. Don't you think she would have wanted this for you? For you to move on, to live a life after her?"

"That's exactly what she told me she wanted." Lydia's voice trembled. "But when she and I stood before that altar, we took a vow that we would belong to each other, always."

"There's a reason the vow is 'till death'. It isn't meant to be a shackle. It's meant to bring happiness, not sadness." Yvonne reached out tentatively, placing her hand on Lydia's arm. "I didn't know Emily. But I know that if she loved you, she wouldn't want you to put your life on hold, to close your heart forever. She'd want you to find someone who makes you happy."

"Even if that means forgetting her?"

"Could you ever forget someone who had such a profound impact on your heart?"

"I already am," Lydia said. "I don't think about her as much as I used to. And my memories of her, they're becoming hazier."

"I understand what that feels like. I've had my fair share of loss. And something I've realized is that we never forget those we lose. While our memories of them might fade over time, what always remains is the way they made us feel. The essence of that person will always live on in our hearts. You won't forget her. Moving on isn't forgetting."

Silence fell between them. Was Yvonne right? But that didn't change the way Lydia felt inside.

"Why don't I give you some space?" Yvonne said. "But if

you need anything, just let me know."

"You've done enough already," Lydia said. "Thank you for letting me know what happened. And for everything else."

"No need to thank me. You're one of us now. We all look after each other."

Lydia gave her a small smile. For Yvonne, displays of sentiment were rare. Lydia couldn't help but feel moved.

Yvonne rose from her seat. Before leaving the room, she paused in the doorway.

"You know," she began. "True love is such a rare and beautiful thing. I consider myself lucky to have found it once in my life. If you're fortunate enough to have a chance at it twice, you'd be a fool to let it slip away."

With that, Yvonne disappeared from the room, and from Lydia's apartment.

Lydia closed her eyes, exhaling long and slow, letting Yvonne's words echo in her mind. She didn't want to let Kat slip away. She wanted to tell Kat how she felt. She wanted Kat back in her arms.

All this time she'd been holding herself back—from Kat, from the happiness that being with Kat made her feel. But Lydia desperately wanted to embrace that happiness. She wanted to find out what a future with Kat looked like.

But even if Kat was willing to forgive her, would she want to be with Lydia? Would Lydia ever be able to provide her with the security that she needed, or would Kat forever feel like Lydia's heart still belonged to Emily?

Could Lydia say for certain that Kat would be wrong to feel that way?

Lydia's eyes flicked to the silver box on the coffee table.

She reached for it, opening the lid carefully, and pulled the collar out, running her fingers along it. Although it felt familiar to her, it was as if it belonged to someone else. Lydia wasn't the woman she'd been with Emily any longer. She'd grown and changed in so many ways. First as a result of Emily's death, then simply due to the passage of time.

She wasn't the woman she'd been with Emily—the tender-hearted submissive and wife—any longer. But she wasn't the harsh Mistress she'd been in all the years following Emily's death either. Who she was now was someone in between, something Kat had helped her discover.

The collar she held in her hands? It would no longer fit around her neck. Although she would always treasure it, she had to stop letting everything it represented hold her back. She was holding on to Emily so tightly that it was stopping her from living her life. Emily would have hated that.

She recalled the words that Emily had said to her in her final days. *Don't bury yourself with me.*

Lydia placed the collar back in the box and closed the lid. It was time for her to fulfill Emily's wish—of Lydia living on after her and finding happiness.

She had a chance to have that with Kat. She needed to seize it.

Lydia grabbed her phone, plugged it into the charger, and waited for it to turn on. She had a phone call to make. It was late, but she didn't care. She needed to speak to the chair of the board, to set up a meeting for first thing in the morning. She was going to give the board an ultimatum. She was going to get Kat's job back, no matter the cost.

And then, she was going to get Kat back.

CHAPTER 26

Kat rolled over in bed and picked up her phone from the nightstand. She had no messages. No missed calls. Nothing. She didn't know why she still bothered checking it. It had been several days now.

And Kat hadn't heard a thing from Lydia.

She threw the phone down onto her bed. She couldn't believe she was here again, holed up in her bedroom, heartbroken and alone. And now she was jobless too.

How could she have been so stupid, letting herself fall again? Had she forgotten how it had felt to have her life shattered by someone she loved? Had she forgotten how badly her ex's betrayal had hurt her? In the aftermath, she'd thought she'd never be able to pick up the pieces of her heart.

But then Lydia had come along, and for a fleeting moment, Kat had caught a glimpse of what it was like for her heart to be whole again.

Something stirred in her gut. She wanted to get that feeling back. She wanted Lydia back.

There was a knock on her bedroom door. "Kat?" Meghan said. "Are you in there?"

Kat grabbed a pillow and covered her ears with it. She didn't want to talk to Meghan. She didn't want to talk to anyone.

Meghan knocked again, harder this time. "Kat? If you're in there, I'm coming in."

Kat stifled a groan and pulled the covers up over her head, burying herself deeper into the bed. Maybe if she tried hard enough, she could fool her roommate into thinking she was a pile of blankets.

As she lay there, she heard the door open, followed by Meghan's bare feet padding toward her. The bed sank down on one side as Meghan sat down on the edge of it.

Meghan sighed loudly. "I know you're under there, Kat."

"Go away," Kat grumbled.

"I will, in a minute. A delivery came for you. Here."

"Just leave it wherever. I'll get it later."

"You're going to want to look at this," Meghan said.

Kat sighed. Mustering all her energy, she pulled the covers down and poked her head out.

"Here." Meghan thrust a box in Kat's direction. It was a long, rectangular gift box, black with a pure white ribbon tied around it.

Kat frowned. "What is it?"

Meghan shrugged. "No idea, but your name is on it. The delivery person said it was urgent."

Kat sat up and took the box from Meghan's hand. She opened it up. Inside was a single long-stemmed rose. She took it out of the box, examining it. It was a deep red color, and impossibly flawless in its symmetry.

Kat's heart skipped a beat. It could only be from one person.

Meghan peered over Kat's shoulder. "There's a card too."

Kat looked into the box again. Sure enough, a small white card sat at the bottom. She opened it up. As soon as she read it, it became clear that the rose was just a means of delivering the message.

I need to see you. I need to make things right.
If you want to see me, be in front of your apartment at 8 p.m.
Lydia.

"I knew it was from Lydia," Meghan said.

But Kat barely heard her. Lydia wanted to see her? After days of silence, she was reaching out?

Megan stood up. "It's only six o'clock now. That gives you plenty of time to get ready. No offense, but you need it. How long have you been wearing those sweats?"

Kat just stared at the note, her chest tightening.

Meghan narrowed her eyes at Kat. "You *are* going, right?"

"I... I don't know." How was she going to face Lydia, after everything that had passed between them? It hurt just to think about her.

Meghan put her hands on her hips. "Katherine Ann Walker. You're my best friend, and I say this with love. If you're not in front of this building in two hours, I'll drag your ass down there myself."

Kat sighed. "I guess I don't have a choice."

"Nope. Now hurry up and get dressed."

A couple of hours later, Meghan practically shoved Kat out the front door.

"Hurry up," she said. "You don't want to be late."

Kat gave her a weak smile. "Thanks, Meghan. I don't think I'd be doing this without you."

"I know. That's what friends are for. Now go."

Kat headed downstairs, her heart pounding. Was Lydia waiting for her, outside? What did she want to say to Kat? What did Kat want to say to her?

But when she reached the street, Lydia was nowhere in sight. Instead, parked right in front of her building in between two old, falling apart cars, was a horse-drawn carriage.

Kat's mouth dropped open. She'd never even seen a horse-drawn carriage in the city the entire time she'd lived here. It had to be Lydia's doing.

Noticing Kat, the carriage driver got out of his seat and opened the door for her, gesturing inside the carriage.

Kat approached it cautiously. It was empty. "Is this for me?"

"Are you Kat Walker?" the man asked.

Kat nodded.

"Then yes, it is."

The man stood to the side, holding the door open, waiting for her. She took a deep breath and got into the carriage. As it took off from the curb, she sat back and watched the streets go by around her. What was waiting for her at the end of the ride? It was almost enough to make her forget about all her inner turmoil.

After passing through what felt like half of the city, the carriage pulled to a stop and the driver opened her door.

Kat stepped onto the sidewalk to find herself standing before a gate. It was the gate to the private park that Lydia had taken her to during lunch that day. It seemed like so long ago now. She pushed on the gate. It was unlocked.

She turned to the carriage driver. "Thank you."

The driver tipped his hat and got back into his seat. He gave the reins a flick, and the horses started back down the street.

Kat stepped through the gate and looked around. The park was deserted, but the path ahead of her was lined with lights, illuminating her way. She headed down the path, crossing the bridge and continuing to the back of the park.

It didn't take long for her to reach her destination. At the end of the path was the elaborate wooden gazebo. Lanterns hung from the roof, and the fairy lights strung around it glowed like fireflies. There was a scattering of flowers and petals all over the seats and the ground.

Standing in the center of it all was Lydia.

Their gazes locked. Lydia's solemn expression didn't change, but even from a distance, Kat could see the affection in her eyes.

Before Kat knew what she was doing, she took a step toward the gazebo, then another, then another, until she was standing inside it, face to face with Lydia.

Her heart stopped. She opened her mouth to speak, but nothing came out.

"Kat," Lydia said. "I'm glad you came." But her posture was stiff, her tone reserved.

Kat looked around her, somehow managing to find her voice. "What is all this?"

Lydia gestured toward the cushioned seat. "Sit. Please," she added.

Kat sat down. Lydia joined her. On the seat between them was a large envelope on top of a small, flat box covered in dark velvet, that was half the size of the envelope.

"What are those?" Kat asked.

Lydia took the envelope and slid a sheet of paper out of it, placing it on the seat between them. "This is a job offer for an executive assistant position. *My* executive assistant."

Kat scanned the page, frowning. "I don't understand. I was fired."

"Yes, from your internship. And I'm so sorry about that. I didn't know. If I had, I would have done something…" Lydia shook her head. "I'm not going to give you excuses. Just know that the moment I found out, I resolved to make things right. I went to the board, and I gave them an ultimatum. I told them I'd resign if you didn't get your job back."

"What?" Kat blinked. "You were going to resign?"

"If I had to, yes. However, it seems the board now considers me too valuable to the company to lose, so they agreed to a compromise. Instead of allowing you to rejoin the internship program, they permitted me to hire you back as my assistant. The position is yours if you want it. I understand if you don't want to work with me anymore, considering how badly I handled everything."

"I… I didn't know you were doing all this. I thought you —" Kat glanced down, avoiding Lydia's eyes. "Last time we spoke, you were so *angry*."

"I know. I need to apologize for how I treated you. And I

need to tell you how I feel." Lydia's hand fell to the velvet box between them. She picked it up and placed it on her lap. "There's something else I want to give you. But before I do, there are several things I need to say to you. Will you hear me out?"

Kat glanced at the box, then back at Lydia. She nodded.

Lydia clasped her hands in her lap, gathering her thoughts. "First, I need to tell you that I'm sorry for how I reacted the other day. It had little to do with you, and everything to do with me. You saw what was in that box. The photos of me and Emily. The collar, *my* collar. Yes, I was Emily's submissive. I lied to you about it because I wasn't ready to share that part of myself with you, the part that belonged to her. You see, when I first met Emily, I was a very different person. I was lost and alone, unsure of myself and my place in the world after my family abandoned me. In Emily, I found that love that I'd always wanted. And our roles—of Dominant and submissive—gave me a sense of security I'd been lacking my entire life."

Lydia's voice wavered. "But after Emily died, it was like I was lost again. I didn't know how to be strong without her. So, I decided to draw strength from her by essentially becoming her. I turned to the familiar world of BDSM, but from the other end of the whip. It was all just an act, a way to cope with the helplessness I felt, but over time, I became the person I pretended to be. I hardened myself, in good ways and bad. It helped me work through my grief, but it also led me to keep other people at arm's length, from friends to lovers. I closed off my heart to love of any kind." She looked into Kat's eyes. "And then you came along."

Kat's stomach filled with butterflies. There was a softness in Lydia's voice, a gentleness that moved something deep inside her.

"From that first kiss, I wanted to make you mine in every way imaginable. I tried to lie to myself, but as time went on, it became impossible for me to deny my feelings. But the harder I fell for you, the more conflicted I became." Lydia wrung her hands in her lap. "I felt as if I was betraying Emily, that by moving on, I'd forget her. So when I saw you, in my bedroom, holding the collar she gave me, I was confronted with all of my fears, and I couldn't handle it, and I took it out on you."

Guilt flashed behind Lydia's eyes. "I'm so sorry for how I reacted. I'm sorry for everything I said to you. My words, they were my own insecurities, my own fears, which I projected onto you."

"I understand, I think," Kat said. "That would have been hard for you."

"It's no excuse for how I behaved. The moment you walked away, I regretted everything. In the aftermath, I was in a bad place emotionally. That's why I disappeared for days. I should have reached out to you instead of pulling away.

"But everything that happened has led me to realize some important things. The most important of them all is how I feel about you. I care about you, more than I've ever let myself admit. I want to be with you. But it feels selfish to want you. You've been hurt before. You need someone whose commitment you won't doubt. If we were together, would you ever believe that I was truly committed to you?

Or would you feel like you only had half of my heart, because of Emily?"

Kat hesitated. "I understand that Emily is a part of you. I'm okay with that, really. But I guess I've been worrying that I'll never be able to live up to her. That I'll never be enough for you because I'm not her."

"Oh, Kat." Lydia gazed at Kat, her stormy eyes now calm and blue as a still sea. "I don't want you to be her. I just want *you*, as you are. You've brought color back into my world. You've made me feel alive again. All this time, I've been holding myself back from you, holding my heart back from you. But I'm not going to do that anymore. Being with you has given me a reason to look into the future instead of looking backward. And the future I dream of has you in it."

She clasped Kat's hand in both of hers. "It's true that Emily will always be a part of me. And I understand if that means you want to walk away. But know that if you stay, I'll give you all of my heart. I love you, Kat. And if you let me, I'll prove that I'm wholly and completely committed to you."

Something flitted inside Kat's chest. "I don't know what to say…"

"Then don't say anything." Lydia took the box in her lap and handed it to Kat. "Just open this."

Kat took the box from her and opened up the lid, peering inside it. Her hand flew to her mouth. "Is this what I think it is?"

Lydia nodded. "I want to make you mine."

Kat looked down at the box again. Inside was a wide, choker-style necklace made of sparkling silver and pure white pearls, with a small heart-shaped lock at the front.

Next to it was a long, thin silver necklace, from which a small key hung. The key was the perfect size for the lock at the front of the collar.

Kat looked up at Lydia. She was too overwhelmed to speak. Instead, she closed her eyes and listened to what her body told her to do.

She put the velvet-covered box down, threw her arms around Lydia's neck, and kissed her harder than ever before.

After what felt like an eternity, Lydia broke away. "That's a yes, I take it?"

"Yes." Kat nodded. "Yes, of course it is. I love you. I love you too."

Lydia kissed her on each cheek, then on her lips. When Kat pulled away, she found a smile dancing on the other woman's lips.

"I have one more surprise for you," Lydia said. "It's in the envelope."

Kat grabbed the envelope and peered into it. There was still something inside, right at the bottom. She turned the envelope upside down and shook it. Out fell two plane tickets.

Kat picked them up and scanned them. "These are for Paris. Next week."

"That's right. Unfortunately, we'll be working for the first few days. Belle Magazine business. But once that's out of the way, we're going to take an entire month off together. We'll be free to spend our days doing whatever we want. Exploring Paris, the rest of France, taking in the sights, doing all those things you've always wanted to do."

Excitement welled up inside Kat. "Really?"

"Really. And one last thing." Lydia took the box containing the collar back from Kat. "I'm going to hold on to this until Paris. Such an important occasion requires a little ceremony, don't you think?"

Kat smiled. "Definitely."

CHAPTER 27

Kat swept into their hotel room and gazed around, wide-eyed. The multi-room suite was almost as big as Lydia's apartment. "This is amazing."

"We're spending an entire month here," Lydia said. "We might as well stay somewhere comfortable."

But Kat barely heard her, having just spotted the balcony. Squealing with excitement, she beelined for the doors, flinging them open wide and stepping outside. The cool evening breeze rushed by as she grasped onto the railing and peered down at the streets below them.

Paris, the city of lights. The place where it had all begun for her and Lydia.

Lydia sidled up behind her and draped her arms around Kat's shoulders. "Do you like it? I got us a suite with a balcony so you could look out and see the city whenever you like."

Kat turned to Lydia. "I love it. And I love you."

"I love you too."

As Kat leaned in to kiss her, Lydia pulled back and put

her finger on Kat's lips. "Patience, kitten. There's something important we need to do first. Stay right there."

Kat waited as Lydia disappeared inside. When she returned, she was holding a small flat box covered in dark blue velvet.

She issued Kat a single command. "On your knees."

Kat fell to her knees before her Mistress, her heart skittering in her chest. She peered up through her lashes, watching as Lydia opened the box and produced the pearl collar, twin to the wrist cuffs Lydia had already given her.

Lydia leaned down and drew Kat's hair to the side. Carefully, she threaded the collar around Kat's neck, fastening it closed with the heart-shaped lock at the front. Once it was secure, Lydia straightened up and took the long silver chain from the box. She slipped it around her neck, the key settling next to her heart.

"You may rise," she said.

Kat rose from her knees. Hooking her finger underneath the collar, Lydia drew Kat close, her body, her face, her lips, less than an inch from Kat's.

"Every time I look at you," she said. "Every time I touch you. All I can think about is how lucky I am that you're mine." She drew the pad of her thumb along Kat's chin. "You're perfection."

In the space of a breath, Lydia's lips were on hers, kissing her with dizzying passion. Desire flickered within her. Lydia's kisses had always taken Kat's breath away, but now they possessed an undeniable sweetness that warmed Kat's heart as much as it set her body alight.

As the kiss grew more ravenous and Kat's hands began to wander, Lydia broke away.

"As much as I like being able to show the world you're mine, I have no intention of putting on a performance for half of Paris."

"Right." Kat had gotten so carried away that she'd forgotten they were on the balcony.

"Let's continue this inside. But first…" Seemingly out of nowhere, Lydia produced a long chain, the leash she'd used on Kat's cuffs that night at Lilith's Den. She clipped it to Kat's collar and gave it a tug. "Come."

As Lydia pulled her inside, Kat followed her closely, not wanting to risk straining her precious pearl collar. However, it proved to be surprisingly sturdy. It was just like her Mistress to choose a collar that was as pretty as it was functional.

She followed Lydia through the living room eagerly. She'd spotted a huge, plush bed in the bedroom on the way in, and couldn't wait to test it out. But instead of heading for the bedroom, Lydia drew Kat through the double doors leading to the dining room. Once inside, she ordered Kat to sit on the edge of the table, giving her a sharp slap on the ass cheek.

Kat sucked in a breath, heat sparking deep within, and climbed onto the table. Lydia grabbed the base of the leash where it met the collar and stepped between Kat's legs, pulling Kat to her.

She traced her fingertips along Kat's collar. "I've been waiting so long for this," she said. "Waiting to claim you. Waiting to make you mine."

Kat exhaled slowly, her whole body throbbing. She closed her eyes as Lydia's lips crashed against hers in a blistering, blazing kiss. She arched back against Lydia, gripping the edge of the table to steady herself. Still holding the leash, Lydia let her free hand roam up Kat's chest, undoing the buttons of her blouse one by one. She flung it open, and glided her hands up Kat's bare stomach, pulling Kat's breasts out of her bra and kneading them firmly. Her fingertips skimmed over Kat's nipples, drawing pleasured moans from her.

Kat shifted her hips forward, the insides of her thighs clenching around Lydia's waist. Kat ground against her, the ache within her becoming unbearable.

"Have you been waiting for this too?" Lydia asked. "Waiting for me to claim you?"

"Yes," Kat purred. "Yes, Mistress."

Lydia pushed her back down to the table and reached for Kat's skirt, snaking her hands underneath it. Kat lifted her hips, allowing Lydia to tear her panties from her legs, and parted her thighs reflexively. She needed her Mistress, now. She needed Lydia to take her and fuck her until she was nothing more than a puddle of satisfied bliss that wholly belonged to Lydia.

But instead, Lydia stepped away and gave her a firm look. *Stay.* Kat obeyed. Lydia rarely needed to give voice to her commands anymore. Had Lydia tamed her, made her into the perfect pet, just like she'd said she would that night so long ago?

The thought slipped from Kat's mind entirely when she saw what Lydia was doing. Somehow, Lydia's leather duffel bag had made its way into the room. From it, Lydia retrieved several lengths of neatly coiled rope and set them down on the table.

Lydia looked down at Kat as she unwound each coil of

rope, a wicked gleam in her eyes. "Remember when I said I wanted to see what you'd look like tied to my dining room table?"

Heat rose to Kat's skin. She was no stranger to bondage anymore, yet just the suggestion of it still made her breath catch and her body pulse with need.

Lydia took a length of rope and grabbed Kat's ankle, tying it to the leg of the table. She did the same with Kat's other ankle, leaving her lower legs hanging off the table's edge, her knees bent and her thighs spread wide, her toes dangling inches from the floor.

But Lydia wasn't done. She took a third piece of rope, raised Kat's arms above her head, and bound her wrists together. "Keep those hands above your head, understand?"

Kat nodded, a part of her wishing Lydia would tie her hands to something so she couldn't move them. That would have been so much easier than having to hold them in place consciously. She wriggled on the table, settling into a more comfortable position. The wood of the tabletop was hard against her hipbones and shoulder blades.

Lydia gazed down at Kat's splayed out body, tracing her finger along Kat's chest. "Now, where were we?"

She reached down to where Kat's thighs met, cupping Kat's mound and letting the heel of her palm graze Kat's hooded clit. Kat bucked desperately, trying to grind against Lydia's hand.

"Hm." Lydia pulled away. "I've changed my mind. You're going to make me come first."

Kat pouted. Lydia had once said that she didn't enjoy causing pain, but the way she would tease Kat, denying her, keeping her on the edge and leaving her hanging—it was utterly sadistic.

But Kat's protests ceased when Lydia reached under her dress and slipped her panties down her long, slender hips, stepping out of them. Kat stared at her Mistress, transfixed, the ache between her thighs growing.

With feline grace, Lydia climbed onto the table and threw one leg over Kat's body, straddling her chest. Kat resisted the urge to squirm underneath her, to bring her hands up and touch her Mistress. Lydia always rewarded Kat for her obedience. She was sure tonight wouldn't be any different.

Lydia lifted her own skirt around her hips. "Let's put that mouth of yours to good use, shall we?"

"Yes, Mistress." Kat's response was automatic now.

Lydia crept forward, lining her hips up with Kat's head, and lowered herself down carefully, hovering just out of the reach of Kat's lips. Kat strained her neck up, her bound hands reaching for her Mistress.

Lydia grabbed Kat's wrists and pinned them down on the table. "Didn't I tell you to keep those hands above your head?"

Oops. "Sorry, Mistress," Kat said.

"Lucky for you, you're about to make it up to me."

Still holding Kat's wrists in place, Lydia lowered her hips down farther, letting her nether lips brush against Kat's mouth. Kat drew the tip of her tongue along Lydia's warm, velvety slit, relishing the taste of her. Lydia sank down even lower, allowing Kat to take her in her mouth completely. Kat let her tongue and lips wander, exploring every little dip and fold between her Mistress's legs.

A murmur of approval rose from Lydia's chest. "That feels incredible."

Kat continued, feasting on her Mistress. By now, she knew exactly how to get her going. She lapped her tongue up the length of Lydia's slit, drinking her in, then dipped her tongue inside Lydia's entrance, savoring her warmth. She painted swirls around Lydia's swollen bud, reveling in the soft gasps her Mistress made in response.

All the while Lydia rocked and ground and rolled back against her, holding onto the ropes binding Kat's wrists like reins. She threw her head back, her breasts heaving invitingly with her every movement. As her pace became more frantic, her thighs began to shake, her gasps turning into moans.

Suddenly, Lydia stiffened, then began to shudder uncontrollably. Her mouth opened in a silent scream, an orgasm taking her. She rocked against Kat's mouth, riding out her climax, until finally, she slumped over, sweaty and spent.

She sat back against Kat's chest, catching her breath. "That was... invigorating. You've earned yourself a little pleasure, I think."

Kat bit her lip, trying to keep her desire at bay. She was even more turned on now than before.

Lydia climbed off Kat and slipped off the table. "Don't go anywhere."

Kat held back a scowl. Lydia was just taunting her now. Bound to the table, her legs spread obscenely, the leash still trailing down her chest, she couldn't go anywhere if she tried. She watched, helpless, as Lydia returned to her toy bag, this time withdrawing her leather strap-on harness, a hard dildo already inserted in it. Lydia slipped it on and secured it around her hips before returning to stand between Kat's legs.

Her hand crept up the front of Kat's thigh, pushing her skirt up farther. "I never did get to fuck you on my desk. This is the next best thing."

Kat's pulse sped up, anticipation and lust rushing through her veins. Lydia grabbed hold of Kat's hips and pulled her closer to the edge of the table, then she took the strap-on in her hand and dragged it up Kat's slit, spreading Kat's wetness over her folds. Her ankles still bound to the table legs, Kat spread her knees out farther, opening herself for her Mistress.

"Eager, are we?" Lydia took hold of the leash, wrapping it around her hand and giving it a tug. "All right, I've tormented you for long enough."

Lydia positioned the strap-on at Kat's entrance. Kat shut her eyes, her breath growing heavier.

Lydia entered her with one slow, deliberate push, burying herself deep. Kat gasped, the empty ache within her replaced by a satisfying fullness. Her feet curled against the table legs and she clamped her thighs around Lydia's hips, holding on as Lydia pumped inside her with practiced ease. Kat jolted and writhed on the table, each stroke unraveling her more and more until she was seconds from coming apart.

"Mistress," she begged.

Lydia pulled out abruptly. "No. Not yet, kitten."

Kat let out a pleading whimper. Lydia ignored it.

"Give me your hands," she said.

Kat held out her hands. With one swift motion, Lydia

untied the ropes binding them, freeing her. Then, she pulled at the leash attached to Kat's collar, drawing Kat to sit up.

She cupped Kat's cheeks in her hands. "I want you close to me," she said quietly. "That's all."

She pressed her lips to Kat's, a furious kiss that made Kat's whole body tremble. Their lips still locked, Lydia reached down and guided the strap-on into Kat again. Kat shifted forward, balancing precariously at the edge of the table, one hand on the tabletop, the other holding onto the side of Lydia's neck.

As Lydia began thrusting again, Kat rocked her hips, matching Lydia's rhythm until they moved as one. Slowly, Kat's pleasure rose and rose, until she was delirious with it, overcome by her need for release.

When she finally came, it was with Lydia's body pressed against her, and Lydia inside her, and Lydia's lips on hers. Kat came apart in her Mistress's arms as ecstasy erupted from deep within, flowing through her body to the tips of her fingers and toes. Lydia held her close, moving inside her, until she was unable to take any more bliss.

As Kat recovered, Lydia untied her carefully. Setting the ropes aside, she swept Kat into an embrace and collapsed onto a nearby chair. Kat wrapped her arms around Lydia's neck, burying her face in Lydia's hair, and let out a contented sigh.

With the collar around her neck and her Mistress's arms enveloping her, the prospect of spending forever like this, with Lydia, no longer seemed like an impossible wish.

EPILOGUE

Lydia stood in the doorway of her office, scanning the room outside it. The Mistress Paris offices were small, and only a dozen people occupied the space. However, that was set to change over the next few weeks.

It had been over a year since that first trip to Paris with Kat. Mistress Paris had opened just a few months ago. Lydia was running it temporarily, splitting her time between the two Mistress offices. Although she liked to travel, the constant flights and long hotel stays were becoming exhausting. Lydia could tell that Kat was exhausted by them too.

She spotted Kat standing nearby, giving instructions to a pair of their brand-new interns in a mixture of English and French. Kat had started lessons long ago, and she'd always been a quick learner. Her talents had been wasted as both an intern and an assistant. But that was about to change too.

Kat turned, catching Lydia looking at her. She handed a file to one of the interns and dismissed them both before walking over to where Lydia stood.

"Is there something you need?" she asked.

"My office, now," Lydia said. "It's urgent."

Kat glanced around before following Lydia into her office. As soon as Kat shut the door, Lydia pulled her over to her desk and drew her into a hot, hard kiss.

Kat rippled against her, sending a surge of lust through Lydia's body. After all this time, Kat still kissed her in that tempting, teasing way, like she was daring Lydia to devour her. For a brief moment, Lydia considered doing just that, right here in her office. That was one of the advantages of the Paris office. No more glass walls. It made stealing moments like this far easier.

Not that she and Kat had to hide their relationship anymore. After everything that had happened—with Kat's firing, with the board—Lydia hadn't hesitated to declare to the world that she and Kat were together. Now, the two of them were free to live their lives together openly. Lydia took advantage of that fact as often as she could.

Kat murmured into Lydia's lips, breaking off the kiss. "Did you really need me for something urgent? The interns are waiting for me."

"This *is* urgent. I haven't kissed you since this morning." Lydia took Kat's hand and drew her fingertips along the pearl cuff adorning her wrist. The collar was a little too obvious for everyday wear, so Kat often just wore the cuff instead. "I wouldn't want my kitten to forget who she belongs to."

"How could I ever forget?" Kat kissed her briefly on the cheek. "But you can't keep kissing me like this at work."

Lydia raised an eyebrow. "Since when do you tell me what I can and can't do?"

A flush rose up Kat's face. "I'm sorry, Mistress. What I'm trying to say is, whenever you do this, I get all worked up, and then I can't get anything done for the rest of the day."

Lydia traced her fingers up Kat's forearm. "Perhaps that's the point. Perhaps I want to keep you on edge all day long so it'll be so much sweeter when I finally get to take you after work."

"We have plans after work, remember? Dinner with Yvonne and Ruby?"

Lydia had forgotten all about dinner. Yvonne and Ruby were flying in this afternoon, Yvonne for Mistress Paris business, while Ruby was simply along for the ride. The four of them had become close friends over time.

"Then you'll just have to wait until after dinner," Lydia said. "I have a new set of restraints I'm dying to try out on you. They're designed to attach to the door." She lowered her voice. "You'd look so lovely strapped to the front door of our hotel room."

The blush on Kat's cheeks deepened. "I'm definitely not going to get any work done now."

"Lucky for you, your boss is in a forgiving mood." Lydia draped her arms loosely around Kat's waist. "I do have another reason for calling you in here. There's something we need to talk about."

"Sure. What is it?"

"When I went back to Mistress's head office last week, Madison and I discussed the issue of finding someone to run Mistress Paris permanently. We came to the conclusion that the best person to do that is me."

Kat frowned. "But wouldn't that mean you'd have to move to Paris?"

"That's right. That's why I told her I'd need to talk to you about it. Not only are you my girlfriend, you're my partner, and my right-hand woman. I couldn't run this place without you. Although, you're due for a promotion. You're already doing far more than an assistant should, and with all the skills and experience you've picked up, you deserve more responsibility."

Kat held her hands up and took a step back. "Hold on. You want me to move to Paris with you?"

"Yes. I was thinking we could get a place together. An apartment, somewhere nearby. Something with enough space for a playroom, perhaps."

Kat stared at her. "I don't know what to say."

"'Yes' would be a good start. But if you need some time to—"

Kat shook her head. "I don't need time. Of course, my answer is yes. There's nothing I want more." She took Lydia's hands in hers. "But are you sure about this? It's a big step."

It *was* a big step, both for the two of them as a couple and for Lydia. She'd become so used to a solitary life, and the fact that Kat worked for her meant that they already spent most of their time together. Moving in together would mean that every facet of their lives would be intertwined.

Was Lydia finally ready to make such a big commitment? Both she and Kat had come into the relationship bearing serious wounds, the kind that didn't disappear overnight. But since then, they'd been through so much together. They'd weathered highs and lows, dealt with every problem life had thrown at them. They'd been each other's comfort through good times and bad. And now they stood together, stronger than ever.

This was a big step for them. A big step for Lydia. But she didn't have a single doubt about taking it. She wanted nothing more than to find out what their future together held.

"Yes," she said. "I'm sure."

A smile grew on Kat's face. "Let's do this. Let's move in together." She wrapped her arms around Lydia's shoulders. "I can't believe it's actually happening. The two of us, moving to Paris, moving in together? This is like a dream. If you'd told me about this a year ago, I wouldn't have believed it."

"Me neither. We've come a long way, haven't we?" Lydia smiled. "Now, I believe you have some interns to attend to?"

Kat waved her hand dismissively. "They can wait."

As Kat leaned in and kissed her again, Lydia reminded herself, as she did every hour of every day, just how lucky she was to have found love again.

ABOUT THE AUTHOR

Anna Stone is the bestselling author of the Irresistibly Bound series. Her sizzling romance novels feature strong, complex, passionate women who love women. In every one of her books, you'll find off-the-charts heat and a guaranteed happily ever after.
Anna lives on the sunny east coast of Australia. When she isn't writing, she can usually be found with a coffee in one hand and a book in the other.

Visit annastoneauthor.com for information on her books and to sign up for her newsletter.

facebook.com/AnnaStoneRomance
twitter.com/AnnaStoneAuthor

Lightning Source UK Ltd.
Milton Keynes UK
UKHW040836270223
417720UK00005B/1014